TRAIL OF THE
SPANISH BIT

**Center Point
Large Print**

**This Large Print Book carries the
Seal of Approval of N.A.V.H.**

TRAIL OF THE SPANISH BIT

DON COLDSMITH

CENTER POINT PUBLISHING

THORNDIKE, MAINE

This Center Point Large Print edition
is published in the year 2003 by arrangement with
Sobel Weber Associates, Inc.

Copyright © 1980 by Don Coldsmith.

All rights reserved.

The text of this Large Print edition is unabridged. In other
aspects, this book may vary from the original edition. Printed in
Thailand. Set in 16-point Times New Roman type by
Bill Coskrey and Gary Socquet.

ISBN 1-58547-354-5

Library of Congress Cataloging-in-Publication Data

Coldsmith, Don, 1926-
    Trail of the Spanish bit / Don Coldsmith.--Center Point large print ed.
        p. cm.
    ISBN 1-58547-354-5 (lib. bdg. : alk. paper)
        1. Indians of North America--Fiction. 2. Great Plains--Fiction. 3. Large type books.
    I. Title.

PS3553.O445T7 2003
813'.54--dc21

                                                          2003051495

INTRODUCTION

I T IS KNOWN that the Spanish, under Coronado, penetrated the American continent as far north as the Central Plains in 1542. History records little other contact in this area.

However, puzzling discrepancies are discovered. A fragment of rusty chain-mail armor turns up in an archeologic dig in central Kansas. Pieces of Spanish-style horse equipment are found along the old Kanza Buffalo Trail.

Words in the languages of the plains Indian tribes are found to have the same sounds *and meanings* as in Spanish. Among some tribes, heavy facial hair was regarded as an indication of royal blood. One noted chief of a century ago was proud of his full moustache.

All these isolated items are inconsistent. They are clearly out of place in time and location. Their occurrence makes no sense at all, unless we concede that there may have been a bit more contact than history records, or in a different manner. The findings are too frequent and too definite to be a logical outgrowth of such chance contact, *unless*—.

I found the Spanish bit in a barrel of junk in northern Oklahoma. The sign said "Your Choice, $1.00." Most of the stuff in the barrel was pretty worthless. Rusty cinch rings, old whiffletree fittings, about like what's hanging on nails in our old barn.

But there was the bit. A ring bit, of Spanish pattern, apparently very old. I bought it and took it home to ponder. It was nearly identical to one I had seen in a museum in Santa Fe, showing the equipment of Coronado's expedition.

How, then, did my bit find its way into a barrel of junk in Oklahoma? And who took care of it for all the intervening years? It was in good condition, and had apparently been protected from the elements.

Several possibilities occurred to me. Perhaps its owner was killed, or his horse killed or captured, the equipment to be plundered by Indians. Possibly he was forced to abandon the animal.

One possibility continued to intrigue me. A few Spaniards were known to have been captured by the Indians along the gulf coast, and later adopted into the tribes. Suppose that this could have happened on the plains. He probably would have been an officer, because most enlisted men traveled on foot. Being a professional military man, he would have a great deal of respect for his equipment, and give it the best of care. As he married into the tribe, his children would have extreme respect for the equipment. In a generation or two, the original use might even be forgotten, but the reverence for the objects so honored by one's ancestor would remain. Family tradition would require continued respect and care.

In the final analysis, we have to say it's all speculation. But, no matter how we daydream, our wildest fantasies would probably pale to insignificance beside the real story that could be told if the Spanish bit could talk.

Don Coldsmith

JUAN GARCIA slumped forward in the saddle, squinted his eyes against the sun, and brooded on the misfortunes that had brought him here to the cursed ends of the earth.

True, he was forced to concede, much was of his own doing. But it had seemed so easy, and so logical at the time. The girl was so young, so lovely in the warm twilight. And her chaperon, the old *doña,* had looked so senile, so easy to confuse and befuddle. The old lady had appeared completely asleep on the bench in the garden, her head resting comfortably against the tree trunk. How could he, Juan, have been expected to know that the old crone was pretending? How could he have seen her smug smile as the young people ran giggling into the dark shadow of the orange trees? And, Mother of God, how could one cadet be so stupid as to select the Commandant's daughter to flirt with in the plaza? He hadn't known that mistake until the girl's father burst upon them with the dog and two burly retainers.

The Commandant had been very charitable, under the circumstances. He hadn't killed Juan on the spot. The young man had even been allowed to resign from the Academy, provided, of course, that he would leave for the colonies in New Spain immediately. Certainly that was far better than an immediate end to the total existence of Juan Garcia. And preferable, of course, to the disgrace that a court martial would have brought on the proud family name.

Juan realized, of course, that he had been saved largely through the prestige of his father. Even the Commandant would think twice before dealing too harshly with the only son of old Don Pedro, patriarch of the Garcias.

Even with this tremendous influence, it had taken much doing, and much gold had changed hands, to acquire for the young man a military commission in New Spain.

His father had insisted that he have the best in equipment. The aging warrior had even bestowed his own sword and armor of fine Toledo steel. The armorer had carefully polished the breastplate and helmet, complete with nicks and scars of successful campaigns in France and Italy. The chain-mail shirt was polished bright by tumbling in oiled sand.

Juan squirmed uncomfortably as a rivulet of sweat trickled from under that same helmet and ran in a tickling prickle down between his shoulder blades. He sighed, shifted his lance, and wondered if his father had any idea how hot the sun of New Spain could be upon a shirt of chain mail.

The gray mare sighed also, and continued to pick her way over the short grass of the rolling prairie. She daintily avoided the small stones and occasional boulders. Garcia spoke to the horse softly and in appreciation of her fine qualities.

Again, his father had chosen the very best of his fine band of Andalusian mares, the beautiful Lolita. This gesture had impressed young Juan perhaps more than any other, but the old Don had brushed all protests aside.

"A man on foot," he advised, limping toward the stable with his son, "is no man at all." His old war wounds were bothering him more every year now. In a way, he envied his irrepressible son the opportunity that shone in the New World.

"He reminds me of myself," he muttered quietly to the groom as they adjusted saddle and bridle. These, too, were the finest the world could afford. Straps and fittings of Spanish leather, with the decorative metal-work by the best of craftsmen. Of the bit, Don Pedro was especially proud. Individually made for the slender muzzle of the dainty Lolita, it was of the ringed pattern. The elder Garcia had theories of his own as to the proper shape and fit against a horse's mouth. The ring around the lower jaw, well fitted, for good control but easy on the horse. And just a tiny copper toggle, on the low curb in the center, to give the horse something to play with. All that remained was the ornamental and decorative ironwork, which the *patron* had left to the discretion of the maker. Delicate lengths of silver chain dangled below slender reins. A light touch was all that was required to instruct and control the gray mare.

Well, Juan had to concede, he was probably a fortunate man, even at that. He was well mounted, well armed. He had been fortunate enough to be chosen for this expedition. A trek to the north, with the promise of wealth beyond one's dreams, in the Seven Cities of Gold.

But there had been no gold. Juan had begun to suspect that none existed. With this came the uneasy suspicion that his captain might be just a trifle mad. He had begun to suspect this shortly after the Capitan had ordered their interpreter strangled.

A pattern had developed. Push a few days north. Capture a few of the local savages and torture them for information about the gold, then kill them and push on. It was becoming obvious to Juan Garcia as well as to others in the command that the captives knew nothing of gold. Probably never even heard of it. Garcia had noticed that none of the captives in recent weeks had any body ornaments made of metal of any sort. Those who nodded and pointed in the direction of the expedition's travel did so only in the hope of saving their own miserable skins.

He was also disturbed by the incident last week. After torture, the Capitan had given the prisoner to the lancers for amusement. The Capitan was very thoughtful of his men. The savage, although limping from the torture, had proved extremely agile. Harried by the priest's dog, the man had still managed to avoid the lances for some time. Even when he was finally transfixed by a lucky thrust, he had grasped the shaft of the weapon. With his dying effort, the native had jerked his tormentor completely out of the saddle. This was still a source of much laughter around the campfires at night.

Juan had seen men die before, usually cringing in terror against the blow of sword or lance. Yet, here was a man, a miserable, tortured savage, who had died with style and bravado. Here had been, Garcia had to concede, a brave man.

All these dilemmas were churning to the young man's mind that morning. He had asked and received permission to go on a short foraging expedition. His father's Toledo sword had been left in the padre's care. Garcia hoped, with a borrowed lance, to kill one of the stupid, hump-backed cattle that abounded in the area. Actually his mission was more personal. He simply needed time to think.

Thinking, however, had only made him more miserable. What would become of the expedition if the Capitan continued the madness? How far north could one travel? Great God, how long it had been since Juan had seen a woman! He half closed his eyes in happy reminiscence of soft curving bodies and tempting smiles.

Therefore he did not see the snake. Wretched creatures, as long as his arm, with castanets at one end, and death at the other. The gray mare saw the threat in time, and leaped sideways, catlike. Garcia was overbalanced before he realized what was happening. A pumpkin-sized boulder rushed up at his face, and he had only partially turned his head when his helmet struck the stone. Lights exploded in his head, he moved slightly, and then sank back into black oblivion.

ℳ 2 ℁

COYOTE, with perhaps a dozen other warriors of his people, squatted in a circle a few paces in diameter around the fallen god. They had been observing the gods for several days before, but this was their first close contact.

Word had reached the People from tribes to the south that the gods were dangerous. They were skilled in torture, for what purpose was not clear. But it seemed prudent to avoid them. There had even been a story for a while that the gods were like a deer with the upper body of a man. That had been pretty well disproved. It was a large animal on which the gods rode. It must be a large dog, Coyote had decided. He could clearly see the thongs that held various articles of the body of the creature. So it must be a dog, if it were a beast of burden. Yet, it was as large as an elk, though with no antlers, and he now discovered another fact. The elk-dog ate grass. He could plainly see it munching. Occasionally it would raise its head and look with large gentle eyes at one or another of the warriors or at the fallen god, and then resume grazing.

The warrior wondered if the elk-dog might be good to eat. Probably. And it certainly had a beautiful skin. Any man would be proud to wear a robe like that. However, Coyote reasoned, it must be more valuable as a beast of burden. Otherwise, the god would have eaten it or be wearing its hide.

Coyote was an observant man, and basically a shrewd one. He knew that the younger warriors laughed at him. He was fatter and less adept at hunting than some, and they laughed at this and the little high-pitched giggle that had earned him his name. He didn't particularly care. He knew that the chiefs valued his judgment, and that his opinions were respected in council. And Coyote had the ability to inject a word of humor into a heated discussion, calmly placing things in proper perspective.

In another culture and another time, Coyote might have been a court jester, or advisor to an emperor, or adjutant to a great general. Among the People, he was Coyote, the wise buffoon, esteemed by chiefs, adored by his wife and children. His lodge always had plenty of meat. Not by Coyote's skill. He certainly wasn't a very agile hunter. But some of the more adept hunters always seemed to be happy to share the results of their proficiency. In return, they received the benefits of Coyote's friendship, his sense of humor, and occasional good advice, when asked for.

Just now, Coyote was disturbed about the god. He had the matter of the elk-dog pretty well solved, he thought, but what of the god himself? The prone figure had lain quietly for several hours now, while the People had crept cautiously closer. He might even be dead. But could a god be dead? Coyote wondered. He had no doubt that a fall like that would have killed a man. He had been closer than anyone when the elk-dog leaped to avoid the real-snake. He had seen the god strike his head on the stone. Should a god not have been able to avoid the fall, perhaps to avoid the real-snake altogether?

And then there was the other thing—the way the god sounded when he fell. He had rattled, like the noise it made when the children would rattle a bone along the dried ribs of a well-decayed buffalo carcass. There was a slightly different sound, too, a ringing sort of sound that was unfamiliar to Coyote. It must have something to do with the hard, shiny skin or shell of the god. This was the first opportunity there had been to study this part of the god's anatomy. The head had a crest on it, like that of some of the lizards on the rocky hillsides. And the god seemed to have a shell like the turtle, front and back. It was shiny, and similar to the look of the crested head—shiny and smooth.

And the god carried a weapon. It looked like a spear. Longer, apparently, and with a longer point, but as he studied it, lying in the grass where it had fallen, Coyote was sure of it. It was even closer to him than the god was, and he moved a little to study its construction and its point. The spear point was very smooth, he noted, and caught the rays of the afternoon sun with a bright glint. Suddenly Coyote realized a startling fact. The material from which the god's spear point was made greatly resembled that of the god's own skin or shell.

Now even gods, he reasoned, would not make weapons of their own skins. So it followed that the shining skins were something contrived to be worn, for ornamentation or protection. The same material must be used for weapons. For that matter, why would a god have need for weapons, he asked himself. What if, Coyote let his mind leap into wild fantasy, what if they're not gods at all, but only men, from a far tribe. If that's the case, the shining skin must be made to be removed, and there would have to be thongs or some sort of fastenings. He moved again, trying to determine how the breastplate was fastened. He thought he could see thongs, but wasn't sure. If he was right, that wasn't a god with a shiny skin, but a man like himself, badly injured or dead. He had half a mind to go down and see. Coyote didn't have quite the courage.

He looked again at the god's head. He was more certain now. The crested thing was a headdress, like that of White Buffalo, the medicine man. He could even see fur below its edges. Coyote couldn't quite see what the fur was attached to. It appeared to grow right out of the god's face. Of course that couldn't be. Maybe his whole idea was wrong. He was just trying to sift around in an effort to see if the boulder had damaged the headdress (or head) of the god. Coyote was becoming very confused. He leaned forward to attempt to see more clearly.

Just then a terrifying event took place that sent all such thoughts scurrying from his head as Coyote himself scurried to safety. For the god gave a long moan, rolled over, and started to sit up.

❧ 3 ☙

THE NEXT THING the god did was extremely reassuring. He vomited. This was very pleasing to Coyote, because it strengthened his suspicions. This creature must be a man, he decided with finality. Surely a god would not be groveling on all fours, gagging and retching and wallowing in his own vomitus.

Coyote settled back on his heels to observe what would happen next. He was pleased with himself, and his good humor was returning. Perhaps some of the other warriors had by this time arrived at the same conclusion regarding the mortality of the invader. But now another problem was sure to arise. What was to be done with him? Kill him?

Surely Hump Ribs, the chief, would call council. He was sometimes a little slow and deliberate in making decisions, but he was a good chief, Coyote thought. Deliberation was a very desirable attribute sometimes. Especially in a situation like this. He had found that there was much to be learned from men of other tribes. Who knew what might be gained from this stranger? Maybe even information about the strange material of his crested headdress. It had prevented his skull from shattering on the rock. How useful.

The god had stopped vomiting now, and sank to a sitting position, head in his hands. He grasped the shiny headdress, and with some difficulty, it seemed, tugged at it to loosen it. He gave a low moan as the object came away, sticky with clotted blood. The effect was ludicrous, as the stranger appeared to remove his head. Gasps from the circle of warriors told Coyote that at least some of the others had not unraveled the mystery until that moment. His lively wit was amused, and he giggled, the little high-pitched coyote laugh.

"Aiee!" he exclaimed, ostensibly to himself. "They also take off their heads!"

A ripple of chuckling laughter ran through the circle, and at this point the stranger seemed to notice the squatting warriors for the first time. His hand darted to his side and he drew a knife, scrambling to his feet to assume a position of defense. This lasted only a moment, as weakness overcame him and he dropped to his knees again.

Probably this weakness saved the stranger's life, for several of the warriors had fitted arrows to bowstrings. Now, however, they hesitated, uncertain. Some looked toward the chief for guidance. Hump Ribs held a hand, palm forward, in a gesture of restraint. Everyone relaxed somewhat. It was a moment of watchful waiting.

The injured man, apparently satisfied that little threat was imminent, sheathed his weapon and staggered unsteadily over to the elk-dog. He unfastened a leather flask from the articles tied to the animal. It apparently contained water, and he took a long draught. Then he sat down on a boulder, exhausted. Coyote noted with some amazement that the black fur actually did grow from the man's face. He must come from a very far-away tribe. Was it to be supposed that all men of his tribe grew fur on their faces? He wondered if the entire body of the man was covered with fur, like that of the black bear. And what of their women? Were they also fur bearing? The entire subject boggled the mind.

Sun Boy was rapidly carrying his torch toward the western horizon now, and the fallen god began to make preparations for the night. Coyote watched closely as the man removed the leather things from around the head of the elk-dog. A long cord, which appeared to be made of twisted thongs, was used to tether the animal.

The man next removed the rest of the equipment from the elk-dog's back, and stowed it against a large boulder. He started a small fire for warmth against the twilight chill. Coyote was interested in his method. Not with rubbing sticks, but with some small objects he took from a bag. One could learn much from this man, thought Coyote.

His thoughts were interrupted as Hump Ribs gestured to the warriors, calling for a council on the small knoll across from the stranger's encampment.

The formal circle was completed and the council fire was lighted. No proper council could be held, of course, without a fire. Hump Ribs opened the discussion. What should be done? Some of the more impetuous warriors favored killing the stranger immediately. At least, others said, we should kill the elk-dog. It looked good to eat, and Hump Ribs' band was somewhat short of meat.

Most were concerned about the danger of leaving the god alive. Coyote had long since decided that the danger afforded by this sick and injured man was minimal. Far more important was the value they might derive from his knowledge. The problem was to convince the rest of the council. Just at this moment Hump Ribs turned to the fat little warrior. This might be the time for the comic-serious advice of the Coyote.

"You have not yet spoken, my brother. What would you have us do?"

"About what, my chief? About 'Heads Off'?" Coyote asked innocently. He paused, eyes darting around the council ring. Chuckles were rippling about the circle, and with satisfaction, Coyote knew that he had made his point. The threat of danger from the wounded man had been eliminated by the simple ruse of ridicule.

"Or about the elk-dog?" he continued. "We could kill it any time. It might be well to keep it alive until we really need the meat."

There were nods of approval around the circle. Coyote settled back as the discussion continued. He had no doubt as to the outcome now. He was doubly pleased when one of the scouts joined the group. This warrior had been following the main force of the strange gods. He now reported that they had appeared to wait for some time for their missing comrade, and had searched the hills. Then, apparently abandoning the search, they had changed direction, turned back to the south, and were camped on Elk Creek. It was suspected that whatever mission had brought them into the country of the People, was now to be discontinued.

After further discussion, it was decided that sentries be posted to watch Heads Off during the night. The other warriors would go to their lodges, only a short journey away, and return with the coming of Sun Boy. Then they would observe the actions of the stranger.

Coyote was quick to volunteer as a sentry. He would have loved to return to his lodge and spend the chill of the prairie night next to his warm wife. He and Big Footed Woman would talk far into the night about these strange events. But that could come later. Just now, he felt obligated to watch the stranger. Coyote had somehow come to think of himself as the protector of this man. Above all, he was curious.

He squatted beside a sun-warmed rock and drew his robe around his shoulders. Even without his sentry duty, there would have been no sleep tonight. Coyote was too engrossed in wondering what Heads Off would do when morning came.

❧ 4 ❧

JUAN GARCIA wakened, after a drugged sleep, to find the circle of half-naked warriors squatting around him in the morning sun. Miserable beggars, he thought. So far, to be sure, they had made no aggressive moves, but he didn't trust them. Especially the little fat one. That one was more curious than the rest. He'd have to watch that one.

His head throbbed when he moved, but survival urgently demanded several things. First he must try to find the rest of the company. Whether that was immediately successful or not, he had to have food and water.

Juan took a few sips of water from the dwindling supply in his flask, and looked around the horizon. To the west was a flat-topped hill that appeared to have a bit more elevation than most. He decided to ride to the top of this prominence. Maybe he could see the Capitan's column from there.

He saddled the gray mare, under the watchful eye of the People, and gathered his equipment. His head pounded painfully as he mounted, but Juan gritted his teeth and endured. His helmet was a problem. One side was badly dented from the fall, and he couldn't wear it. It would be a simple matter for the armorer to straighten the dents, but for the time being, he had no alternative but to tie the clumsy thing to the saddle. He doubted that he could have worn it anyway, with the goose-egg-sized lump behind his right ear.

To his amusement, a number of the savages followed him as he moved off. Or rather, they flanked him, on both sides. They moved in an easy, ground-eating dogtrot that kept pace nicely with the comfortable gait of the mare. Perhaps it would be better to outdistance them, he thought. He touched the gray into a canter, but the experiment was rapidly terminated for two very good reasons. First was that his aching head wouldn't take the pounding. Second, it didn't seem to work, anyway. The savages dropped behind a bit when he really pushed the mare, but as he slowed, they rapidly closed the interval. Even the fat one. And, Mother of God, he couldn't gallop all the time. He decided to tolerate their company, since he didn't seem to have much choice anyway.

The view from the hill was disappointing. He could see far over the rolling, grass-covered prairie, but could see no sign of his company. To the east in the distance, he could see a wandering line of tall trees that would be alongside a creek or river. In the bend of this creek he saw a number of the strange, conical leather tents used by the savages. Probably those of his present escort, he assumed. They were now squatting easily a safe distance from him, awaiting his next move. Juan wondered what that was going to be.

His searching gaze swung to the north, and there he made out the dark forms of a dozen or more of the hump-backed cattle. Well, since he had nothing better in mind, might as well try to kill one of those for food.

He hadn't brought any supplies, since he hadn't expected to be away from the column for long. Surely they'd look for him, and he'd have meat for the company when they found him. He turned north, unwittingly farther away from his comrades, who had already assumed him dead.

The buffalo were grazing in a level, grassy meadow. Coyote and his people had seen them also, and a couple of runners were sent to the village to carry the word. Here was the meat they needed. A hunting party started immediately, followed by the women, who would do the butchering of the kill.

Garcia, followed by the handful of warriors, reached the meadow first. Coyote's people were anxious as they topped the hill overlooking the buffalo. This crazy stranger might frighten the animals and send the badly needed meat far away. Perhaps they should have killed him after all.

They watched, fascinated, as Heads Off prepared for his charge. The useless helmet was dropped to the grass, and the long spear was readied.

Garcia had been considered expert with the lance at the Academy, and now his skill would be tested. He selected a fat young cow, and maneuvered into a good position. As he began his run, the bison raised their heads and started at a deceptively clumsy gallop for parts beyond. The mare gained rapidly on the small herd, and soon spotted the animal that her rider had selected. Aiee, thought Coyote. The elk-dog can certainly run! And Heads Off, he noted, had chosen the best of the meat. How much easier than the tedious attempts to surround a chance individual that might stray from the herd.

Fascinated, he watched as the elk-dog, ears flat, drew rapidly alongside the running cow. At exactly the proper moment, the long shiny point of the lance thrust into shaggy hide. A clean thrust, just behind the ribs, forward and down into vital areas of heart and lungs.

The cow slowed, stumbled, and fell, coughing blood from nose and mouth. Coyote was pleased. The other warriors could now see that it was more useful to have Heads Off alive than to kill him. Never had he seen a buffalo killed more easily. The team of Heads Off and the elk-dog had done a superb job of acquiring meat, and had caused it to appear so simple.

Juan Garcia, meanwhile, was not feeling that it had been so easy. His head was throbbing again from the exertion. He wasn't sure he could manage to secure and cook some of the meat. He stiffly dismounted, hacked a sizable chunk from the hind quarter of the cow with his belt knife, and walked, on foot, for the shade of a tree at the edge of the meadow. He found a pack rat's nest of sticks in the fringe of brush at the hillside, and used it to start a small cooking fire.

He was just propping sticks with strips of meat over the coals when the hunting party arrived. There was animated conversation between his erstwhile escort and the newcomers, and much looking and pointing in the direction of Heads Off and the elk-dog. The gray mare was now grazing contentedly nearby.

Then the women arrived, at first shy and suspicious, afraid of the stranger some hundred paces away, but tempted by the fresh meat. Gradually they became more confident, chattering and laughing at their work while the men lolled around in small groups, visiting amiably. Some of the women, Juan noticed, were reasonably attractive, with long legs and strong willowy bodies. By Christ's blood, he cursed to himself, what am I thinking? I've been in this Godforsaken country too long!

By the time the young man had cooked and eaten part of the meat, and cooked and stored the balance in his saddle bags, the butchering was complete. The women straggled over the hill and out of sight in the direction of the village, carrying their spoils. He began to think about his next necessity. Water. The expedition of the Capitan had usually had no trouble locating a spring or stream by sending out several scouts.

Sometimes, however, they'd been pretty dry for a day or two. He couldn't risk that in his present weakened condition. He had to find water, and recover sufficiently to start an intensive search for his people. He couldn't ride in all directions. He remembered that the skin tents he had seen were near a stream. Of course, the savages would know where to find water. He'd follow them for tonight, and then start his search tomorrow.

Garcia stepped into the saddle, and started over the hill, past the stripped bones of the cow. Trotting easily at each side was his ever-present escort. Much later, he realized that he had forgotten his discarded helmet. And, Christ, how his head was aching again.

OYOTE AND THE PEOPLE watched the stranger closely that evening as he followed them to the village. He seemed harmless enough now. He did, Coyote noticed, know enough to move upstream from the village to go to water. Heads Off and his elk-dog both drank deeply and the man filled the waterskin he carried, and tied it to the animal again.

He then remounted and rode to a level spot on the hill overlooking the village. His dusky observers moved a few yards away and hunkered on their heels to watch his preparations for the night.

By Christ's blood, he swore to himself, I'm certainly sick of their staring. At all times there were at least two or three of the savages just squatting and staring. If he moved, they followed. When he stopped, the watchers stopped too and instantly assumed the odd squatting position of rest. He was amused, but irritated. The thought occurred to him that it might be amusing to test his skill with the lance by taking a run at one of the savages. However, his horse was already unsaddled, and his head still ached. Also, he told himself, perhaps so near to large numbers of the creatures, it might be well to be discreet. True, they had shown no animosity so far. They had even seemed pleased at the windfall of meat that his foray had provided.

The young man watched the activity in the village from his vantage point on the hill as the shadows

lengthened. He was most impressed by the appalling smell of the place and by innumerable dogs that wandered among the skin lodges. Small children stared in his direction, but did not approach, apparently cautioned by their elders. His ever-present sentries had been reduced to two this evening. He judged that they were assigned guards to watch his movements. One of them was the fat one. He watched that individual and found that they were staring at each other with fixed gaze. It became a contest. Who would outstare the other? Somehow it became an important achievement not to blink or lower the gaze. His eyes burned and his head ached, and he longed to put his face in his hands. Damn the savage, he thought, why won't he lower his eyes to his betters?

Coyote was rather enjoying the contest. This strange Heads Off became more and more a human being, as one watched him. He was reacting to the staring game like any other man. Coyote had found a straight level gaze very effective in dealing with people. Of course, he had also discovered that the stare was very disconcerting and irritating to some men. These he had learned to placate in a most clever way. To drop one's gaze was a universal sign of weakness, but Coyote occasionally wished to terminate the game, and he must do so without causing the other any undue irritation or loss of face. So, he utilized his trademark, the coyote giggle. He did so without moving his gaze, but in a carefree fashion, to allow the other to relax and yet save face.

Coyote now utilized this technique and the tension

relaxed. Garcia, still irritated, moved around, settling for the night, placing his equipment carefully, and covering his armor with his saddle to keep off the rusting effects of the heavy prairie dew. He built a fire for warmth, and drew his saddle cloth around his shoulders. Great God, how his head hurt! I have to find the company, he thought miserably, but I'm too sick to ride. He was paying dearly for the effort expended to kill the buffalo. Weakness had nearly overwhelmed him before arriving at the savages' camp. Even now, his aching head throbbed with every heartbeat. And he must have more shelter than a saddle cloth. The weather had been uncommonly fine, but it was bound to rain any day. The young man realized how precarious his position had become, but was too tired and sick to do anything about it. He rolled miserably in the saddle cloth, and curled up as closely to the fire as seemed practical.

At the end of his watch, Coyote threaded his way back to his lodge, where Big Footed Woman sleepily raised the edge of the buffalo robe to invite him to bed. He divested himself of weapons, leggings, and breechcloth, which he hung from various projections on the lodge poles. He slid gratefully between the soft warm robes and snuggled close to his wife.

Coyote's relationship with his woman was unique. He knew that many of the warriors considered their women little more than useful possessions. Somehow, perhaps from his own wise mother, he had grasped the idea that an able woman could be more. An intelligent companion to share one's thoughts.

"I have learned more about Heads Off, the god," he began, curling closely against her warm body. "He plays the staring game much like other men."

"The staring game?" she gasped. "You have been that close to him? You must be careful, my husband!"

"It was nothing." He shrugged carelessly. "He is only a man, like me. And I have learned another thing. He does not grow fur upon his entire body, like the black bear."

"How do you know this?"

"I watched. He removed some of his garments in order to empty his bowel. And," he paused for effect, "his butt was as bare and shiny as mine. Nearly as shiny as yours, woman!" He circled her hips with an arm, and playfully patted that portion of her anatomy.

Big Footed Woman giggled softly and snuggled closer to him, responding appreciatively to his playful caresses.

ᘄ 6 ᘇ

GARCIA did not ride to seek his own people the next day, or the next. He lay miserably next to his fire, rising seldom. The throbbing in his head swelled to a crashing thunder when he moved. Once when he walked around a bit to try to locate fire-wood, he realized that he had overexerted. Dizziness washed over him in a nauseating wave, and he dropped to all fours and vomited. How long, he wondered, could he go on this way? The rest of his life? Which, incidentally, wasn't going to be very long if something didn't happen to improve the situation. He was out of meat again, and really didn't feel like engaging in another buffalo hunt.

The warriors who had been on assignment, apparently to watch him, had now dwindled to one or two. They had become careless. He had the impression that perhaps they were now assigned only to report when he finally died. Damn you, he thought, I'll not give you that satisfaction.

The following morning, Juan Garcia felt slightly better, and managed to ride out into the prairie far enough to find a tough old buffalo cow. He was reeling in the saddle by the time he made his kill, but managed to hack off a chunk of meat without quite finding it necessary to stop and vomit. No sooner had he quit the carcass than the women descended on it like locusts again, stripping it clean. My God, he noted, they use every part of the thing.

The young man made his way back to his camp near that of the savages. Or rather, the little gray mare did. Garcia was only semiconscious when he arrived, tired, sick, dizzy, head throbbing. He sank exhausted beside his little fire and fell into a fitful doze.

He awoke from a dream in which a professional torturer was squeezing his head with an infernal machine. Each turn of the screw brought a new throb of pain between the temples. Starting up, he came to reality to see a scrawny dog from the camp trying to steal his hard-earned meat. A whack from the butt of the lance sent the animal scurrying, tail between legs.

As he moved about, building up his fire, Garcia realized that the wind had changed. A definite chill was in the air, and a line of towering white-topped clouds was building up in the north. The rain he had been dreading seemed to be fast approaching. The young man managed to cook most of his meat before darkness fell and a steady drizzle settled over the prairie.

Mother of God, he wondered, teeth chattering, why didn't I keep the buffalo skin today? At least it would have kept him dry. He had forgotten that he had probably been too weak at the time. His saddle blanket was soggy, and even his fire seemed in jeopardy. He threw on a few of his precious sticks and the fire blazed up again. Garcia dozed.

A furry shape awakened him this time. He had extended a hand as he moved in his troubled sleep, and had come in contact with something hairy. The lance butt swung again, but stopped short. The scavenging cur was not the cause of his rude awakening. By light of a flickering flash of lightning, he saw a folded buffalo robe beside him. He looked quickly around, but saw no one. Even the fat little warrior, his almost constant observer, was gone.

Garcia unfolded the robe and spread it over his head and shoulders, listening to the patter of rain on its surface. Warmth began to return to his body, and his chattering teeth quieted somewhat. Someone, he mused, had done him a great favor. Perhaps even saved his life. He had heard of persons whose lungs filled with fluid from being cold and wet. They sometimes died, unable to breathe. But who had placed this robe beside him as he slept? He thought of the fat little savage, the one who irritated him so. Could it be his? That one had been near just before his last sleep. Garcia chewed on a strip of his hurriedly cooked meat and pondered. He pulled the robe more closely around him, and noticed, by feel rather than sight, a flaw in the furry surface, near one edge. It had a crescent shape, a slit in the soft tanned leather. Some accident or injury to an old, well-used robe, he supposed. Then he suddenly remembered that he had seen that defect before. A slit in the edge of an old robe. He felt it again, to make sure. Yes, it was as he remembered. And he now remembered where he had seen it. The last time he saw that defect, it was in a robe that was thrown carelessly across the shoulder of the fat little savage. That's odd, he mused. He was the one I thought the most dangerous. Just curious, maybe.

The young man curled luxuriantly inside the warm fur of the robe and drifted off to the best sleep he had had in nearly a week.

WITHIN a day or two Juan could feel his strength returning. He could walk farther, and began to think perhaps he could even ride in search of his comrades. If he couldn't find them, he could head southward in the general direction from which they'd come. Eventually, he should reach the settlements of New Spain. Of course, that might take many weeks, and the season was late. He didn't know what to expect in this part of the world. Snow and ice? The weather would be better farther south, he was sure. Maybe he'd better try it. He had his buffalo robe now, in case he encountered a storm or two.

The day after the rain he had attempted to return the robe to the little fat savage. That one had refused, smiling and pointing first toward Garcia, then making motions of spreading a garment over the shoulders. The young Spaniard had understood that he was expected to keep the robe.

He began to plan his departure. He killed another buffalo, and saved larger quantities of the meat, planning to use it while traveling. He considered the skin, but realize the futility of trying to do anything with the heavy, green hide. He had no idea how to prepare such a thing for use. It was abandoned to the women.

Garcia was primarily worried about water. His waterskin would hold only about enough for one day, and none for the horse. He would have to find water almost daily. He was still struggling with this dilemma when the People prepared to break camp.

Hump Ribs was a chief who enjoyed creature comforts. His lodge was large and comfortable, and was well managed by his several wives. The chief was the one who made such major decisions as to the moving of the camp. His decisions frequently hinged on comfort. In this case, two comforts. He was looking ahead to the unpleasantness of the winter season. It was much preferable to spend that season a bit farther south, in milder climate.

The other comfort involved more aesthetic feelings. Several dozen people in close proximity produced a large amount of refuse-rotting meat scraps, fought over by the dogs. Excrement from those same dogs, and human excrement. Sanitation was poor, but basically unnecessary. When the camp became foul-smelling enough to offend the nostrils of Hump Ribs, he simply ordered a move.

When Juan Garcia awoke that morning he noticed the extra bustle and confusion. It was some time, however, before he realized that the skin tents were coming down. The covers were folded and tied, and various possessions stowed in rawhide bags. By midmorning the first family units were threading their way over the hill, heading south.

Garcia was amazed to see the dogs used as beasts of burden. In some cases, packs were simply lashed on the dog's back in the manner of a peasant packing a burro. Yet there was another method used here. A couple of the long slender lodge poles were lashed alongside the shoulders of a dog, trailing in the dust behind. Then packs and bundles were placed on small sticks tied across between the two poles. The dogs seemed able to pull tremendous loads in this fashion.

Garcia's thoughts were reaching rapidly ahead now. The savages were heading in the general direction he desired to travel. Undoubtedly they knew where to obtain water. It would be essential for so large a group. So, he reasoned, why not travel with them or near them to take advantage of their knowledge?

Shortly after noon, the last of the People straggled over the hill, leaving a meadow littered with bones, discarded lodge poles, cast-off articles of buckskin, and stinking refuse. Behind them, at a little distance, rode an incongruous figure on a horse. He was clad in chain-mail shirt and body armor, but without a helmet. He carried a lance.

⚜ 7 ⚜

B Y THE END OF A WEEK OF TRAVEL, no one seemed to think the presence of the stranger even unusual. He stopped when they did, and camped nearby. Once when a band of buffalo had been sighted, Garcia had ridden out to try for some provisions. On a whim, he had decided to try to drive some of the beasts toward the savages, largely out of curiosity to see what would happen. He managed to drive several of the big animals toward where warriors waited hidden in the tall grass. To his amazement, their stone-tipped arrows and short spears dispatched four buffalo in rapid action. He was impressed by the bravery of the men. They would stand firmly before a charging bull, then jump aside at the last moment and strike the soft flank as the animal brushed past.

The young man had one more shock that day. He realized with some surprise that he was now regarded as a hero. The savages smiled at him, and little children ventured much closer than previously. He was a trifle irritated. He hadn't intended to become their benefactor and was a little embarrassed that his act of simple curiosity had turned out that way.

A few days later, after time had been taken to prepare and store the meat from the kills, the band moved on. Little game was now seen, the grass was poor, and Garcia became anxious. He had had no way to store any but a few days' provisions. He had already discovered, to his disgust, that the strips of broiled meat started to decompose rapidly after a day or two in saddle bags.

He soon saw the savages' answer to the problem of fresh meat. A woman stepped out toward where a group of dogs lay resting in the evening sun. She held a morsel of food in her left hand and made squeaking noises with her lips. Several of the animals ran toward her, and one fat dog met his end at the swing of a club. In a short time the skinned and gutted carcass of the dog was roasting before her cooking fire. Garcia decided he wasn't hungry yet.

The next evening, after preparing her family's meal, Big Footed Woman set aside a generous portion on a piece of rawhide. Like wives and mothers everywhere, she was deeply indoctrinated with the desire to feed those men with no food.

"Take this to Heads Off," she told her husband. Coyote was pleased, and lost no time in trotting over to the nearby camp of the stranger. He approached without hesitation by this time, and laid the offering near the seated youth.

"Eat!" he said, accompanying the word with the universal hand signal. "Eat!" he picked up a morsel and proceeded to demonstrate. Garcia was initially slowed by thoughts of his first attempt at roast dog, but found the first bite acceptable and ventured more.

"Eat?" he questioned, speaking the word and using the hand sign.

Coyote was delighted. "Eat!" He nodded eagerly.

Then he picked up the waterskin nearby. "Water," he said and signed. "Water." He pointed to the nearby stream and made the sign again. "Water."

"Water," repeated the other, nodding.

"Drink," with the appropriate sign, head tilted back.

"Drink," answered Heads Off.

Coyote giggled, pleased at having established communication.

A young woman walked past, gathering firewood, and nodded to Coyote, her flowing hair falling across her shoulder.

"Woman," said Coyote, indicating with his hand the sign language symbol, that of flowing loose hair across the shoulder. His pupil nodded again.

"Woman," he answered, pointing to another girl. Both men laughed, enjoying the game. Garcia picked up his lance, with a questioning look.

"Spear," answered Coyote, making the hand sign. The younger man repeated the word and sign. He was reading the hand signs quite easily, and suddenly realized with surprise that the signals constituted a sort of language. By means of a few simple hand motions, a sort of conversation could begin. He pursued this further, asking the signs for various nearby objects. The young man concentrated on the hand signals, rather than the guttural syllables of the strange tongue.

Garcia quickly found that he could almost guess the hand signs for many familiar objects. The buffalo robe, for instance, must be described by a motion of covering the shoulders. Of course! The little native had used that gesture previously. Juan pointed to the robe, made the sign, and was pleased to find that he was correct.

Then a thought struck him. He pointed to the horse grazing nearby and looked, questioning, to his tutor. Coyote stopped short, spread his hands in bewilderment. There was no sign for the elk-dog, since one had never been seen before. He pondered a moment. The other man grasped the source of his dilemma. Finally Coyote decided on an appropriate sign. He raised his left hand, palm toward himself, fingers extended. With his right hand, he made the sign for man, index finger and middle finger pointing downward to resemble legs. Then with these legs he straddled the edge of the other hand. Of course, Garcia understood, a man astride a horse. Both men chuckled. They had found a new word sign.

The darkness crept across the prairie, and still the two men sat, enjoying the new, mutually acquired skill. A coyote on a distant hill heralded the rising moon with his chortling song. Another answered from nearby.

"Coyote," said the bearer of that name, pointing into the night. He then pointed to himself.

"Coyote," he giggled. Garcia laughed aloud. He could understand perfectly. Coyote. What a logical, descriptive thing. The man's giggle sounded exactly like the distant animal's cry.

"Juan Garcia," the young man said, pointing to his own chest.

"Wahn Gar-zee-ah?" the other rolled the unfamiliar syllables over his tongue. "Gahr-zee-aw?" After several attempts he shook his head in despair.

"No," he said positively. "You are 'Heads Off'!"

It was many weeks before Juan Garcia understood the significance of his new name. As he rolled into his robe to prepare for sleep, he found confused thoughts whirling in his brain. Ever since he had stepped off the ship onto the soil of New Spain, he had held a preconceived notion. He had regarded the inhabitants of this new world as savages, little better than animals. It had never occurred to him that they might have feelings and emotions and even a sense of humor. The little warrior, "Coyote," he called himself, had demonstrated that. The realization had come to Garcia this evening, that heathen though they might be, these were human beings. People. And this in turn brought the young man to another thought, warm and pleasant as he dozed off. He hadn't taken time to realize it, but Mother of God, how he'd missed having someone to talk to.

༄ 8 ༄

DURING THE NEXT DAYS, the People continued their southward migration. The weather began to change somewhat. There were occasional temperature changes at night that made Heads Off draw the buffalo robe closely around him and roll closer to his fire.

Long lines of geese, calling loudly to each other in flight, were occasionally seen in the clear blue sky. The colors of the maturing prairie grass changed from green to gold and reddish. In the canyons and gullies that occasionally wandered through the gently rolling hills, the hardwood trees began to show brilliant colors of fall foliage. Ripening nuts and acorns held the attention of the People for a few days in one area, as they gathered and stored the crop. Fat fox squirrels, too, found the bountiful harvest attractive. It was possible to vary the diet of the People with a welcome treat of broiled squirrel.

Garcia, though impatient to be on the move southward, endured these delays. He was doing practically no cooking now. At the next buffalo kill he had made after establishing communication with Coyote, a new procedure had been established. As he dismounted and approached the carcass with his knife, the wife of Coyote had intervened. She had reminded him of Maria, the housekeeper in his long-ago childhood, shooing him gently aside and signing that she would do it.

And oddly, the other women respected this arrangement. It became common knowledge that Heads Off hunted for the lodge of Coyote. Big Footed Woman was accorded the privilege of first choice of the meat from the kill. Only then did the others move in to complete the butchering of the carcass.

In this way Garcia found more time to think and to observe. Big Footed Woman or one of her children brought his food each time she prepared a meal for her family. She was a handsome woman, Heads Off noted. Probably not much past thirty, about the age of her husband. Her feet weren't really so big, he observed upon learning her name. But she was long and graceful, with a calm, proud demeanor and a purposeful stride. She had kept her figure well, despite several children. The oldest was a girl who appeared cut from the same pattern as her mother. Just blossoming with the first soft curves of womanhood, she was called, he had learned, the Tall One.

Heads Off had, for convenience, made his camp each night beyond the perimeter of the native encampment, but near the lodge of Coyote. The evening conversation between the two men became almost routine. Coyote found the younger man an apt pupil. He grasped the sign language very rapidly, and soon attempted words and phrases in the guttural language of the People. Their discussions were a mixture of signs and spoken language, often simultaneously.

"What are the boys doing?" Heads Off asked one evening. He had been observing a game played by a group of youngsters.

One of the boys climbed on the back of another and brandished a stick. They then ran at a third child and struck him with the stick. It was very puzzling.

"They are playing 'Heads Off,'" Coyote chuckled. "The boy with the stick is yourself," he pointed, "and he rides upon one who is the elk-dog. They kill the buffalo."

The young man was flattered, and was immediately struck by the similarity to his own play as a child. He had pretended to be various of the young caballeros around the village where he grew up. He laughed, pleased at the insight.

He noticed that some of the games were more organized. Youngsters of a little older group, approaching adolescence, were frequently seen practicing with their weapons. Some of the warriors often gave advice and instruction. One man in particular seemed to be a favorite of the youngsters. He was called by the unlikely name of Mouse Roars. Heads Off had been impressed by this man's handling of the short spear as well as the bow and arrow. His ability was apparently well respected in the tribe. He was a slender, athletic individual, with large ears and a sharp-nosed face. His mild manner and calm, kindly demeanor was in sharp contrast to his physical prowess. Heads Off decided that must be the reason for his name. He asked Coyote about it.

"Why is this man called 'Mouse Roars'?"

"Why not?" Coyote shrugged. "That is his name!"

Some of the young men seemed more proficient with their weapons, of course. Among these was Long Elk, the son of Coyote. He seemed to have inherited his mother's graceful agility and height, as well as his father's keen mind and sense of humor. He was quick to learn, and immediately took a great interest in the elk-dog. He and his friend Standing Bird, son of Mouse Roars, at first brought big armfuls of fresh grass to offer the animal. As Heads Off tolerated this, they ventured to groom the glossy hide with a handful of dry grass. Soon they worked as confidently around the little mare as if they had been horsemen all their lives. Her owner even allowed them to lead her to the stream for water, and eventually to sit on her back occasionally. Heads Off thought both the youths had possibilities as first-rate horsemen. This struck him as ironic. There wasn't another horse in a month's journey.

Heads Off was also interested in preparation of food for storage. This knowledge might be useful on his journey back to his people. Strips of buffalo meat were cut from the carcass and dried in the sun on racks made of sticks. The resulting leathery chunks could be chewed, soaked in water and cooked, or made into pemmican, which was a mixture of the dried meat pounded to a meal and mixed with tallow. Sometimes nuts and berries were added. The resulting substance was stored in lengths of buffalo intestine. Very like sausages back home, Garcia thought.

He watched the preparation of skins for lodge covers, clothing, and various utensils. This appeared to be a constant labor for the women. However, they seemed to take a great deal of pride in the quality of their work. Extensive decoration on the leather shoes, shirts, and dresses consisted of dyed porcupine quills. Garcia thought some of the intricate designs quite attractive. Some appeared to have great religious significance.

Each day Garcia thought about his coming journey. He was sure that he could pack enough pemmican on the horse to enable him to travel without stopping to hunt. When the time was right, he would ask Coyote about it, and barter somehow for a supply.

Meanwhile, as long as the People were still heading in the right general direction, he'd simply accompany them. This day-to-day existence had been working out pretty well until one warm afternoon when Hump Ribs called a halt. Here, he announced, the People would spend the winter. It was an ideal spot, a level grassy meadow with sheltering hills on the north and a clear flowing stream.

Garcia realized that the time was drawing near for his departure. He'd spend a day or two collecting his supplies and then be on his way. His horse was in good condition, and his headaches had now practically ceased. He'd talk to Coyote tomorrow, he thought as he prepared for the night.

It was only an hour later that the storm struck.

❧ 9 ❧

THROUGHOUT THE DAY the People had been watching a low line of clouds behind them. Garcia had seen it, too. He had regarded it as simply another of the passing cloud formations which had been the weather pattern for past weeks. A thin cloud bank would build up in the northwest, sweep across the plains and out of sight to the southeast. This occurrence had become so commonplace, every three or four days, that he had failed to notice that this cloud bank looked different. Heavier, thicker. To further confuse the deceptive situation, the afternoon had been balmy. Almost hot. A light gentle breeze blew from the south, and the young man was lulled into a false sense of security. He was enjoying the springlike day.

The People knew. There was a general rush to estab-

43

lish the camp. The lodges were erected rapidly, pole frameworks tilting toward the sky and the semicircular skin covers raised to position and laced. Garcia had already noticed that the doorway and smoke opening at the top always faced to the east. This, apparently, to take advantage of the prevailing winds. Smoke flaps could be adjusted with long poles to make the smoke "draw" better. Very clever, he thought.

While he was watching and relaxing, the wind changed. There were only a few minutes, it seemed, when the south breeze was quiet, waiting. Then it returned, soft little tentative gusts at first. It was from almost the opposite direction now, gaining in intensity as the storm front rolled in from the north. The temperature dropped abruptly, chilling the body even before the setting sun was obscured by the advancing cloud bank.

Garcia hurried to his selected camp site, and kindled a fire near the limestone outcropping. The scattered rocks would give some degree of shelter. A drizzling cold rain started to fall, and the young man spread his buffalo robe over his head and shoulders. He squatted with his back against a boulder, which still retained a little of the sun's heat. Icy spray blew around his ankles and up under the robe. Gusts of the now chilling wind whipped sparks from his fire. These were quickly extinguished by the heavy rain.

As the darkness began to fall, the temperature continued to do likewise. Soon the rain had turned to sleet, and Garcia was not only cold and miserable, but somewhat worried. How cold would it get before the storm abated? Teeth chattering, he tried to adjust the robe around his body to better achieve protection. The heavy, wet skin slipped from his numb fingers, and before he could grab the flapping thing, his left shoulder was drenched.

He shuddered, genuinely cold now. The driving sleet was rapidly extinguishing his fire. He glanced at the horse, standing with rump to the storm and tail between her legs. Her back was humped against the cold. He wondered if he could snuggle against the horse's body for warmth. Just as he had nearly made up his mind to try it, he saw a figure approaching from the lodges.

"Come!" Coyote beckoned, and stooped to help gather the few possessions of the other. Turning, he led the way at a trot, back to his lodge, glancing behind only to be sure the youth was following.

The men stooped to enter the doorway, and stepped inside. Coyote's wife hurried over to tie the strings that held the opening shut against the weather. A cheerful fire burned in the center of the circle, and the lodge was warm and comfortable.

Coyote pointed to a pallet of skins at one side. He stepped over to assist in arranging the various articles of the guest's belongings. Most of the small articles he hung from projections on the lodge poles over the bed. It now appeared to be the assigned sleeping place of the young visitor.

Coyote clapped his hands to call the attention of the children. They were already staring, big-eyed, at the visitor, from the periphery of the circular room.

"Hear, now," their father began, pointing to the equipment they had just hung on the poles. "These things are the medicine of Heads Off. This," pointing to the Spanish bit, "is the very strong medicine that enables Heads Off to control the elk-dog. When it is placed in the elk-dog's mouth, it must do anything he desires."

Exclamations of awe escaped the children.

"This," he continued, pointing to the chain-mail shirt and the body armor, "is also powerful medicine. It protects him from harm, as a shield does in battle."

He paused to make certain they were properly impressed.

"Now," he continued, "Heads Off is to be a guest in our lodge. None of you must at any time touch the medicine things of Heads Off."

Frightened looks from the large dark eyes indicated that there was little danger of transgression.

Garcia had been unable to follow all of the discourse. He was unfamiliar with the concept of a personal strength or power or magic, the "medicine" an individual possessed. However, he did grasp the general theme. The children were being forbidden to touch his equipment. He had already noticed the strong sense of ownership of personal property among these people.

He looked around the room. This was the first time he had entered one of the skin lodges. It was about five paces in diameter. The fire burned in the center of the circle, and smoke rose steadily, straight toward the apex of the cone. Directly across from the doorway was a pile of furs and robes that apparently formed the bed of Coyote and his wife. Around the periphery were other, smaller pallets, the sleeping areas of the children. There was a sort of leather curtain that hung from waist height around the entire circumference of the circle, forming a vertical wall. Garcia realized that this lining serve to minimize the draftiness at the outer edges. He immediately learned another use, that of storage space. Coyote lifted the edge of the lining and motioned to put the saddle in the space behind. The youth could see a variety of the rawhide bundles he had noticed each time the tribe moved. It occurred to him also that food storage in winter would be improved. There would be much less spoilage in the cooler area next to the outer cover and separated from the warm interior.

Big Footed Woman interrupted his thoughts as she offered him meat. Garcia leaned his lance against a lodge pole and sat cross-legged on his pile of skins to eat. The storm howled and sleet rattled on the skins of the lodge, and the family of Coyote began to make preparations for the night. Garcia, grateful for the warm shelter and the food, began to relax.

Suddenly, a disturbing thought occurred to him. With the weather in this cursed country liable to sudden change, it would be completely out of the question to travel. Even with the weather as uncommonly fine as it had been today, it would be possible to become trapped in the open by a situation like this. It could easily be fatal.

And I'm already trapped, he told himself with a sinking feeling. I'm a prisoner of circumstances here with these stinking savages. And I have to spend the whole winter here.

ᴥ 10 ᴥ

ONCE HE HAD FAIRLY WELL RESIGNED HIMSELF to his predicament, Garcia found life not too unpleasant. The storm had been short-lived, most of the snow and sleet melting in the sun by the following noon. The People bustled around the encampment, making preparations for the winter. A period of warm, sunny weather followed.

The young man marveled at the changeability of the prairie weather. Without realizing it, he was learning a great deal about the social customs of the band. He was fascinated by the informal yet structured learning procedure accorded the boys. Nearly every day the youths could be seen practicing use of their weapons. They also contested with each other in running, jumping, wrestling, and swimming. Mouse Roars or some of the other warriors were always on hand to supervise. He noted that, in contrast to his own youth, the youngsters were never struck by the instructor. They were often praised, sometimes ridiculed, but physical punishment seemed completely absent.

Mouse Roars' instruction group, he learned, was called the Rabbit Society. All boys were expected to belong, although no actual punitive measures were employed. Apparently manhood was achieved by the demonstration of skill in the hunt. After successfully demonstrating this skill, a young man was graduated into the Hunter Society, Coyote told him.

Girls, too, belonged to the Rabbit Society, he was surprised to find. However, their instruction ran more to the domestic skills. Both boys and girls learned the dance together, with an old man beating a rhythmic thump on the drum, and singing. An occasional girl joined the boys of the Rabbit Society in practice with the bow and spear, or with the throwing sticks. These stout, well-balanced clubs could be used to secure rabbits, and an occasional squirrel, he noted with interest. Some of the girls were unusually adept with the bow, and running races were popular with both sexes. A challenge to run would be instantly taken.

Many of the youngsters, both boys and girls, could swim like otters. Nearly every warm afternoon, the wide clear pools of the slowly flowing river would be filled with happily shouting children. Sometimes they were joined by adults. The pastime appeared so inviting that Garcia ventured to try it himself, in a sheltered pool well upstream from the camp. He was very cautious, since he had never learned to swim. Actually, his acquaintance with water had been rather infrequent. Bathing had not been a major part of his upbringing. He found that the idea rather appealed to him. The savages, he decided, had habits of personal cleanliness at least as adequate as his own. However, he was still appalled at their lack of public sanitation. There was no apparent effort on the part of many to deposit body excreta out of the beaten path.

Nearly every evening, he and Coyote would carry on a discussion in the lodge. Big Footed Woman and the wide-eyed children would listen solemnly, but never interrupt. The men would sit on the beds of buffalo robes, and lean back against back rests, made of willow sticks laced together. The semi-reclining position was quite comfortable.

Occasionally, there would be a "smoke." The first time this occurred was quite a surprise to Garcia. In the lengthening shadows of evening, after the meal had been eaten, Coyote stepped outside the lodge.

"Hear me, my friends," he shouted. "Come and smoke!"

Men began drifting from other parts of the encampment, and soon there were a dozen or more seated around the periphery of the lodge. Initially, there were many curious or cautious glances at the guest. Soon, however, the short red-stone pipes were being passed, and the air of the lodge was made blue with pungent smoke. Garcia had never acquired a taste for tobacco, but ventured to try the pipe passed him by his host. He coughed at the mixture of sumac, willow leaves, and tobacco in the pipe. The other guests smiled politely.

Conversation was limited to recounting tales of great hunts and humorous episodes of the past. A smoke at the lodge of Coyote was always enjoyed, as conversation was lively, and there was much laughter and good fellowship. How very much, Garcia thought, like a bunch of his father's old military cronies, recalling old battles over good red wine.

He learned another thing in the course of the next few weeks. He had always regarded the savages as completely devoid of facial hair. Now, he discovered, this was not entirely true. Some men did indeed have a countenance as smooth as a new baby's rump. Others were possessed of some rather patchy facial growth. By custom these sparse hairs were plucked out, using clam-shell tweezers. This, he realized, was because they had no metal knives or razors. It would be next to impossible to shave hair with a flint. Usually the women of the lodge assisted where necessary. The result was that all the men of the People had smooth faces. This was an important part of the care of one's appearance, as much so, it appeared, as the careful braiding of the hair.

Garcia was mildly amused. His own beard had grown, early and thick. The custom of the time was toward full beards, especially in the military. They could be roughly shaped with shears or even with one's belt knife. He had trimmed his hair and beard several times on the present campaign by means of simply hacking off the longest portions with his knife. Primarily, the beard must be kept at least short enough not to be caught in one's chain-mail shirt. He had occasionally had the experience of having a few hairs become entangled in the metal links. This could be a rather startling sensation, as well as a nuisance.

He imagined it would feel very similar to pluck one's beard with the clam shells. With a facial covering as dense as his own, it would be little short of torture.

There came an occasion when Coyote informed him that they had been summoned to the lodge of the chief, Hump Ribs. The young man involuntarily looked with dismay at his now tattered clothing. A few weeks before he would have given no thought to his appearance before an ignorant savage. Now, somehow, it had taken on new importance. As if she saw his dilemma, Big Footed Woman rummaged behind the lodge lining and drew forth a package. She smiled and handed him a pair of buckskin leggings and a soft breechclout like those of the men and boys of the People. From another container she took a pair of hard-soled moccasins and signed him to put them on.

The young man had long since overcome any modesty he may have had. Living with a group of people in such close quarters certainly precluded privacy. He changed his clothes, and found the new attire not at all uncomfortable. It did, he admitted, chafe him in rather strange places, but was tolerable.

Coyote dressed up a bit for the occasion, he noticed, putting on an ornamental breastplate of tubular beads that appeared to be made of bone. After some thought, Garcia took down his chain-mail shirt and glanced at his host. Coyote smiled and nodded. The young man slipped the jingling armor over his head and settled it around his shoulders. It was uncomfortable, even through his linen shirt. He had forgotten how uncomfortable chain mail could be.

The two men took up buffalo robes, and Garcia carefully draped his robe over a shoulder in the same manner as his host. They threaded their way through the encampment toward the lodge of Hump Ribs. It was easily the largest in the camp, and was decorated with geometric designs and a stylized painting of a warrior thrusting a spear at a huge buffalo. They paused outside.

"We are here, my chief," called Coyote.

The curtained door parted, and the two men stepped inside. A young woman allowed the skin to fall into place, and tied the thongs. She motioned them forward.

The general arrangement of the lodge was similar to that of Coyote's. The fire burned in the center of the floor. Shy wives and children peered cautiously at the stranger.

And directly across from the doorway, in the place of the master of the lodge, was a pile of the finest robes. On this pallet sat the chief of the People, the stern-visaged Hump Ribs.

"Come in, Coyote, Heads Off," the chief's deep voice, rumbled. He indicated with a wave of his hand a pallet beside him.

The two guests seated themselves, Garcia slightly nervous. Women moved silently around the fire, bringing food to the three men on pieces of rawhide that looked to Garcia like very thin boards or shingles. Several of the food items were new to the young man.

One he found especially good was a thick mash of some sort, apparently flavored with suet. Horn spoons were furnished with which to eat. The substance tasted rather like squash, which puzzled him greatly. Where would they have obtained squash? Coyote, his erstwhile tutor, was of no help. Neither knew the other's word for "squash."

Talk during the meal was limited to remarks about the weather, which had been uncommonly fine, and comments on the availability of game. This subject was used by the chief to bring Heads Off into the conversation.

"We are very grateful to you, Heads Off," the chief spoke slowly and directly to the young man for the first time. "You have helped us much with the hunt. We are pleased to have you spend the winter with People."

His guest was able to understand most of the speech, aided by sign language from Coyote. He nodded, unsure of the proper way to respond.

"From where do your people come?" continued the chief conversationally. With the help of Coyote, the young man clumsily constructed his answer.

"We have come from a far place," the young man stated with difficulty, "beyond the Big Water."

"Yes," nodded Hump Ribs, "I have heard of the Big Water. Is it true that one cannot see the other side?"

The concept of the ocean was completely foreign to the People. Second- and thirdhand reports simply failed to convey the meaning of a really large body of water. None among the People had ever seen a lake that one could not walk completely around in a day. Garcia lacked the language skills for further description, and the subject fell rather flat.

The elk-dog was discussed briefly, Hump Ribs noting what a great help in hunting the animal was.

"Are elk-dogs also eaten by your people?" he inquired. He received the quick answer that it was not the usual thing.

"Perhaps it would be bad medicine among his people," Coyote ventured. Garcia nodded. He was becoming more familiar with the concept of "medicine." That was a close enough interpretation for the present. Besides, if the savages thought some sort of medicine taboo existed, this would mean an additional protection for the horse. He was still somewhat uneasy when he was out of sight of the animal. He just wasn't sure yet how far the respect for his property rights would go.

As the guests were leaving, the chief spoke a quiet aside to Coyote. "You must take Heads Off to meet White Buffalo," he suggested.

So it occurred that Coyote was designated a task of major proportion. The visitor must gain the approval of the medicine man.

The clever Coyote planned his strategy carefully. First he called on White Buffalo alone, and related to the old medicine man the instruction of the chief. The other nodded.

"I think the medicine is very powerful," observed Coyote, "but Heads Off has used it only to help with the hunt. Perhaps I can persuade him to bring his medicine so that you may examine it."

White Buffalo, dignified and reserved as was his custom, found it difficult to remain calm under the circumstances. What a rare privilege, he thought, to be able to examine the medicine objects from a far land. He had already heard exaggerated tales of the hunting exploits of Heads Off and the elk-dog. The aging medicine man, with no young apprentice ready to step into his moccasins, had begun to feel threatened. Perhaps the medicine of the newcomer would prove stronger than his own.

It was with mixed emotions, anticipation and dread, that he carefully dressed himself and painted his face. The headdress of his office was made ready, and the old man prepared his various herbs and powders and rattles and bones.

At the appointed hour the two visitors approached. Heads Off, at the suggestion of Coyote, was dressed in his chain-mail shirt and body armor. He was leading the saddled mare, but tied her outside the lodge as the medicine man's wife admitted the two men. They stood blinking for a moment as their eyes adapted from the bright sunlight to the dim of the lodge. Bundles of drying herbs hung from the lodge poles.

Garcia saw the figure of the medicine man opposite the door, standing proudly to observe the visitors. His ceremonial facial paint shone brilliantly in the fire-light, and the young man looked with astonishment at the headdress. It was made from the skin of a buffalo's head and neck. The horns were attached and rose on either side of the priest's head, while the skin of the neck and hump hung down over his shoulders like a cape. And to the young man's amazement, the entire costume was of purest white. He had not grasped the significance, until now, of the medicine man's name.

Coyote was speaking, "—and has been among the People for many summers. Each medicine man gives his name and the medicine headdress to the young man who will take his place. White Buffalo makes medicine for us before every hunt, so that we may kill the buffalo."

The old medicine man drew a pinch of some sort of

plant material from a pouch and threw it on the fire. Fragrant smoke arose, and he began his medicine ceremony. Garcia watched, fascinated, as the old woman began a rhythmic beating on a small drum. White Buffalo produced a long staccato roll with his turtle-shell rattles, and began to step around the fire in the maneuvers of the dance. He bent forward, mimicking the slow swaying gait of the buffalo. Every motion conveyed the same impression. The pawing of a front foot, the swing of the massive head. White Buffalo must have spent his entire life, Garcia realized, studying the behavior of the animals.

The thoughts of the old man were much along the same lines as he danced around the fire. He remembered well his apprenticeship. How many hours he had spent in the stooped position, with a calf skin over his shoulders and head. He had been able to mingle freely in the herd, undetected. On several occasions in the past, when meat had been scarce, he had been able to help with his medicine. The one year, for instance, ten summers back (or was it eleven?), when the People had made their biggest kill of all time. He had to admit that was largely luck, but it had taken a bit of planning, and more than a little medicine.

The large herd had been grazing in an area that made it relatively easy for him to move among them and herd them quietly in the direction of his choice. And at the proper moment, the People had jumped from behind the rocks, yelling and waving their robes. What a spectacular sight! Dozens of the great animals, pushing, shoving, frantically trying to escape, falling to their deaths at the bottom of the cliff, pushed by those behind.

What a great feast there had been, what huge quantities of dried meat and pemmican! None of the People had been hungry for many moons. They had also traded many robes with other tribes.

But in recent years, he had feared his medicine was weakening. Becoming old and motheaten, maybe, like the precious white buffalo cape. There had been times when the hunters were unsuccessful. And he, White Buffalo, had sometimes been physically unable to accompany them on the hunt. He had tried to make medicine before the hunters started forth, but he was uneasy about it. He was certain it wasn't as effective that way.

And now, this stranger had appeared on the scene. The entire tribe had been able to talk of little else but Heads Off, the elk-dog, and the wonderfully effective medicine for the killing of buffalo. Clearly, this man could be a threat to the prestige of the medicine man. He must find some way to eliminate this threat.

ᕫ 11 ᕬ

AS HE FINISHED THE DANCE, the medicine man knew that he was at a time of decision. He was still a bit undecided as to his next move. He would be expected to make public an opinion on this newcomer, and he wasn't sure yet what that opinion would be. It would be foolhardy to oppose the medicine of Heads Off. The tribe had already realized much benefit from the extra buffalo kills. On the other hand, White Buffalo could feel the threat to his prestige.

Perhaps Coyote would be of help. Surely his friend Coyote would not bring about a situation harmful to his medicine and his prestige. He had watched Coyote as a youngster; what a thinker he had been. There had been a time when White Buffalo thought perhaps Coyote might become his apprentice. The young man would have been a good medicine man. Perhaps even a great one. But he had had many other interests. A restless, inquiring mind, the old man recalled. Coyote had refused the strict discipline of the proposed apprenticeship, and had taken other directions. And he was, White Buffalo recalled with amusement, just a trifle lazy.

The two had remained friends through the years, and Coyote had continued to show a great deal of respect for the older man. The medicine man had, in turn, been pleased to see his young protégé become a respected man in the council.

Now, he considered, Coyote might have a plan in mind. He would take a neutral position until he had a chance to see. The drumbeat ended, and the medicine man removed the white headdress and placed it carefully in its protective cover. Then he turned expectantly to Coyote, waiting.

Coyote's insight had made him aware of the dilemma of the medicine man. In fact, he had spent a lot of time in thought concerning the problem. He must help White Buffalo save face, and yet admit the great advantages of the newcomer's medicine.

He thought the answer might lie in the fact that the two medicines were different. Both powerful and useful, but different. He had great respect for the medicine man's knowledge of herbs and plants and their usefulness. The old man also had an uncanny knowledge of the buffalo. He could predict their migrations and always seemed to know where the herds might be. He could judge just the right time to fire the dry prairie grass in the spring. Lush new growth, starting in the burned prairie, attracted the herds to the easier grazing.

Now, thought Coyote, Heads Off provides an easier way to secure these buffalo. Their medicine does not conflict, it works well together!

"Come, my friend," he beckoned to the medicine man, "we will show you the medicine of Heads Off." He led the way outside, to the waiting horse. White Buffalo had not yet seen the animal close at hand.

"This, of course, is the elk-dog," Coyote began. "Heads Off controls it with this," he indicated the bit in the horse's mouth, "a powerful medicine." White Buffalo nodded, impressed. "This enables him to sit on the elk-dog's back, and it must do whatever he wishes."

Garcia, understanding most of the discourse, was again impressed with Coyote's grasp of the situation. It was pretty accurate. The control of a horse actually does depend on the bit in its mouth, he observed. And this, he grunted, is pretty big "medicine."

The medicine man was impressed. He examined the horse closely.

"What," he wanted to know, "does this have to do

with buffalo?"

"Nothing!" Coyote was pleased. His strategy was working. "This part of his medicine is only for the elk-dog. The rest of his medicine," he turned and thumped on the body armor of the young man, "is only for his protection."

He related the incident in which Heads Off had fallen and struck his head. Only the medicine, he pointed out, had prevented him from being killed. Coyote had many times regretted that the helmet had been lost. He hoped to try for its recovery when the People moved that way again.

White Buffalo felt better. Perhaps there was no threat after all. Coyote was continuing his discourse, driving home his final point.

"So," Coyote finished, "this has been very good for the People. Your buffalo medicine has brought them to us, and the elk-dog medicine has helped us to kill them. The People have more food than we have had for many winters."

White Buffalo was pleased, and invited them back into his lodge for a smoke. Heads Off, though unsure about the intricacies of the conversation, perceived that the tension had relaxed, and that somehow he had been accepted. Still, he thought, it will be good in the spring to return to my own kind.

The young man was also experiencing another kind of tension. He had noticed from his early days of contact with the People that some of the women and girls were quite attractive. He had been wondering ever since about the possibility of a liaison. His emotions were further stirred by the living conditions in the lodge of Coyote. In such close proximity, it was impossible not to overhear the nightly activity from the bed of Coyote and Big Footed Woman. The sounds of rhythmic motion and the sighs of pleasure were very frustrating to the young man as he lay sleepless in his buffalo robes.

Probably the best-looking young woman in the camp, he noticed, was the Tall One, daughter of Coyote. She had been very shy around him, glancing from beneath long dark lashes, but dropping her gaze quickly when their eyes met. Garcia was strongly attracted to her, but uneasy about attempting to promote any contact with his host's laughter. At least, not the sort of contact he had in mind.

He had also noticed an attractive young woman who lived in a nearby lodge. She had an easy, flirtatious smile, and a swing to her hips as she walked that was very stimulating to him. She had repeatedly given the young man a broad, inviting smile when they chanced to meet, and Garcia was planning how best to expedite the next steps.

Her name, he found out, was Flowing Water. Appropriate, he thought. That was suggested by the low, seductive trill of her laughter. He would try to encounter her "accidentally" on a wood-gathering mission outside the camp, and then see what ensued. Her seductive smile already told him it would not be difficult.

When the opportunity came it was completely unexpected. He had been tending to the needs of his mare and was returning to the camp. There was a path through the thick willow brush along the stream, probably originally made by the numerous deer. In places the growth was so heavy that the path resembled a tunnel, with branches arching overhead. Garcia was picking his way through the thickest portion of the passage, when he noticed a figure ahead in the deep shadow of the overhanging willows. For a moment his defenses were alerted, but then he realized it was a woman, and he recognized Flowing Water. She smiled and stepped aside for him to pass. However, he noticed immediately that the girl had chosen a rather narrow spot on the path. There were several wider areas within a few steps, where passage would have been more convenient. Instead, she had deliberately placed herself at the side of the trail, not really out of the main pathway. Furthermore, she stood facing the passageway, not turning aside. Her full bosom thrust forward, making no pretense. Garcia slowly stepped past her, turning to face her as he brushed past her body.

For a moment they touched, face to face, with lips only a short distance apart, and the girl leaned forward to press against his chest with a quiet, seductive little laugh. His hands found her waist and pulled her closer, her hips thrusting eagerly toward him as he placed a kiss on the full, ripe mouth. Her armful of firewood fell scattering to the ground and soft arms encircled his neck.

Garcia glanced quickly around and remembered a hidden clearing he had noticed under the arching willows nearby. Both were breathing heavily, and he took the girl by the hand and led her from the main path toward the shady nook. They sank down on the soft grass and he pressed her to him again.

Just at this inopportune moment came a rustling in the willows and a chatter of childish voices at play. Flowing Water leaped to her feet and disappeared into the bushes, arranging her skirt as she ran. Garcia sat, frustrated and dazed. Never mind, he thought, there will be another day, my little flirt. He wasn't sure whether she had specifically sought him out, or whether her flirtatious manner was aimed at any available man. No matter, the result would be the same. He'd see to that later.

One afternoon not long afterward he was lounging outside the lodge and talking with Coyote. They had moved their willow back rests out into the warm autumn sunshine, and were relaxing comfortably. Suddenly there were shouts and screams from down by the river, and Flowing Water appeared, running toward her lodge and crying. She was pursued angrily by a young man, who kept striking at her with a heavy stick and shouting at her. A crowd began to gather, and Coyote and Heads Off joined them. The young warrior had caught up with the girl and grabbed her arm, shouting a rapid torrent of words. Garcia was puzzled, but could not understand so fast a dialogue. He touched Coyote's arm, making the hand signal for a question.

"Her husband caught her rutting with another man," answered Coyote in a matter-of-fact tone. "Flowing Water has always been a bad one. Now he may do anything he wishes with her."

The man began to beat his wife systematically, across the shoulders, back, buttocks, and legs. She screamed and begged, falling to her knees, but the beating continued. Garcia impulsively started forward to help her, but was restrained by Coyote.

"It is none of yours, Heads Off," he stated calmly.

Another man thrust his way through the crowd, shouting angrily.

"That is her brother," explained Coyote. "He thinks the husband is too severe."

The beating stopped and the two men angrily stood shouting at each other. Suddenly the husband turned and seized his wife by the hair, pulling her head back. Quickly he slashed across her face with a sharp object, a flint knife or spear point. Blood spurted from her cheek and she screamed as he threw her to the ground.

"Now," he shouted at his brother-in-law, "she will be too ugly for any man to lie with!" He whirled and strode into his lodge.

A gasp and a murmur came from the crowd, then silence, except for the sobbing of Flowing Water. Both hands covered the mutilated face, and crimson ooze trickled between her fingers. The People began to shuffle away, returning to normal activities.

"He was really very good to her," explained Coyote, as they strolled back to the lodge. "He might have cut off her nose or ears. He could also drive her away on the prairie."

"But what will happen to her now?" the shocked young man blurted.

"She will probably stay with him," answered Coyote.

"She could return to her own family if they let her, but they are poor. Nobody else will marry her now that her husband has shamed her." He nodded to himself. "She will stay with him, I think. He is a good husband."

How fortunate, Garcia was thinking, that he hadn't gotten mixed up in the middle of that. He wasn't sure what might happen to the other party involved in the triangle. He certainly didn't want to find out in the wrong way. Maybe, he decided, it would be better if he could hold his desires in check until he could return to his own people. There, at least, he knew the rules. And he certainly didn't want to leave any portions of his anatomy here on the prairie at the insistence of an irate husband's flint knife.

ᘰ 12 ᘺ

GARCIA was badly shaken by the incident involving an unfaithful wife. Not that he was unused to violence. But this was simply not the sort of thing he had expected. In the colonies of New Spain farther to the south, there were native women to be had practically for the asking. He resolved to find out more about marriage customs, or whatever passed for marriage, among the People. Actually, sexual customs, to be more accurate.

His information was by observation, augmented with cautious questions. When a young man wanted a girl, he learned, he offered her father something of value. Robes, ornaments, or weapons. How odd, Garcia thought. In his own homeland it was the opposite. The girl's parents furnished a dowry. This method of the People seemed almost like buying the girl from her father. Still, there were differences. The women, though burdened with constant hard work, seemed to demand a great deal of respect among the People. He noticed several of the warriors who had a relationship like that of Coyote and Big Footed Woman. A warm, friendly companionship. Some of the men had more than one wife, usually men of prestige and affluence such as Hump Ribs.

Among the very young who married, it was quite customary for the new husband to move into the lodge of his wife's parents. There the newlyweds would live until able to construct their own lodge. Garcia could see definite disadvantages.

During such a discussion in the lodge, one of the younger children interrupted.

"Heads Off," the curious youngster asked, "among your people, do the women grow fur upon their faces?"

"No, little one," the young man chuckled, tousling the boy's hair, "the women are almost as pretty as your sister!"

Tall One blushed furiously, and shooed the younger children from the lodge. Both her parents chuckled quietly as the girl busied herself over the cooking fire. She was cooking a stew of dried meat and corn, and Heads Off began a conversation with her. He had wondered how cooking could be accomplished without pots, pans, or kettles, and had learned since moving into Coyote's lodge. Now, with Tall One cooking at the moment, he suddenly became even more interested in observing the process. Big Footed Woman had several round smooth stones half the size of a fist which she called "cooking stones." Near the fire she had carefully scooped out a small pit and lined the cavity with rawhide. It would then hold a quantity of water. Meat or vegetables would be added while the cooking stones were heating at the fire.

Tall One sprinkled drops of water on the stones from time to time. When the drops produced a hissing sound, she took the stones with heavy tongs made of green willow, and dropped them into the stew. By adding hot stones from time to time, and removing the cooler ones to the fire, a steady boiling was induced. The best cooks, Garcia judged, would be the women who knew just when to add or remove the stones.

Suddenly a thought occurred to him. The girl was cooking corn! Where did corn come from? He recalled the squash at the lodge of Hump Ribs. Where on earth were the People acquiring vegetables?

He asked Tall One, and was unsure of her answer. It contained words not understood by the young man. Puzzled, he turned to Coyote.

"We trade for them with the tribe down the river," explained Coyote. There was a little difficulty communicating the concept of barter, but by means of sign language and a few questions, Garcia verified that he indeed understood. Robes and sometimes meat or pemmican were exchanged for corn, beans, and squash. Coyote pointed to newly acquired bundles of dried squash, the rings threaded on a thong and hung from the lodge poles.

"Haven't you noticed the women going down-stream?" Coyote asked.

Garcia had merely assumed that they were gathering wood or buffalo dung for the fires. He had been so pre-occupied with his own thoughts that he had paid no attention.

"There is another band nearby?" he asked, surprised. "Some of the People plant corn?"

"Of course not," replied Coyote, rather irritably. "These are not the People. The People are hunters."

Now Garcia was completely confused.

"There are others who are not the People?"

"Yes," Coyote nodded, now understanding the con-fusion. "There are many who are not the People."

"Then only Hump Ribs' band are the People?"

"No, Heads Off. There are many more. There are several bands, like that of Hump Ribs. But all of the People are hunters, not like these others, the Growers. Heads Off will see the other bands of the People when we go north in the summer to meet them for the Sun Dance."

No chance of that, my friend, reflected Garcia. When the People go north, Heads Off will travel south. Then, startled, he realized that he had thought of himself as Heads Off, not as Juan Garcia. Mildly irritated, he lounged back on his bed. He still didn't quite under-stand the distinction between "the People" and other people.

"Coyote," he tried a new approach, "where did the People come from?"

"From inside the earth. Great Spirit sat on a hollow

cottonwood log. He rapped on it once with a stick, and First Man crawled through the log from inside the earth. He rapped again, and First Woman came through. They were naked, and he showed them how to kill animals for food, and how to use the skins for garments and for lodge covers. He showed them how to make fire with the sticks, and how to make medicine to please the spirits of the wind and rain and the buffalo. And he told them they must have many children to use all the wonderful things he had shown them."

Coyote was speaking eloquently now. The wide-eyed children stared fascinated at their father, enjoying the familiar story. The storyteller turned.

"Tell me, Heads Off," he inquired, "where do your people come from?"

"We come from a far land across the Big Water," the young man began. Coyote shook his head and raised a restraining hand.

"No, no, Heads Off, I know that. But I mean in the old, old, very old times."

Garcia had never thought much about it. Now he searched his memory for something that would give him an idea where to begin. At the beginning? A phrase crept into his consciousness. *In the beginning God created the heavens and the earth.* The instruction of the padre, long ago. He took a deep breath.

"In the beginning, God," he paused, looking for words, "the Great Father, made the earth. Then he took a handful of the earth and shaped a man, and called him 'Adam,' and breathed life into him. Then he saw that he needed a woman, and he made him a woman, and called her 'Eve.' " He'd leave out the part about the rib, he figured. "Then he put them in a—uh—a place, where there was every kind of animal and plant, and told them to use it."

Garcia decided to skip the part about the snake and the apple and all, but felt he should go just a little further.

"Then, much later," he continued, "Great Father sent his son to show us how to live."

"It is the same with us," Coyote nodded eagerly. "Great Spirit sent Sun Boy to guide us with his torch."

The women announced the meal, and the conversation came to an abrupt end. But later, as he lay in his robes watching the dying embers, a thought occurred to Garcia. A rather bothersome thought. Only now had he begun to realize the significance of Coyote's chance remark, "It is the same with us."

Granted, there were some minor differences. Granted, he had omitted some of the details. He wasn't sure why. He had tried to convince himself it was because Coyote wouldn't understand. But now, he wondered. Did Coyote already know what he, Garcia, had just begun to realize?

That in the conversation they had had before the meal, he and Coyote had been telling each other the *same story*.

ࣷ 13 ࣷ

THE WINTER passed slowly for Juan Garcia. He was impatient for spring so that he could begin his journey back to his people. He had abandoned any further thought of romantic liaison. He could wait, he decided, until his return to the colonies. His daydreams were often of warm, dusky cantinas, where good wine flowed and graceful dancers whirled to the music of his homeland. Often he woke in the night with the pungent smoke of the lodge fire in his nostrils. Sometimes he imagined for a moment, in awakening, that it was the smoke of the familiar fireplace in his childhood room, with servants quietly tending the hearth.

One of his major concerns was for his horse. Lolita grew a thick furry coat against the weather, and seemed to tolerate the low temperatures in good condition. However, Garcia worried about the availability of food for the animal. His father's horses had always spent the more inclement weather in the big stable, and had been fed the finest of hay and grain through the winter months. He worried about the mare's ability to forage. When the grass dried on the prairie hillsides, she had continued to graze to a certain extent. However, she seemed to spend more time in the fringes of timber available to her. He had stopped picketing the animal. She stayed fairly close to the familiar area of the camp, apparently seeking human companionship. There was little lack of that companionship, as either Long Elk or Standing Bird, or both, were constantly near her. Garcia was amused at their devotion. Several of the younger boys sometimes hung around at a distance, enviously watching the two favored ones. The elk-dog was obviously an important interest in the life of the People.

When the first deep snow fell, silently in the night, the People withdrew into their warm lodges, except for a venturesome few youngsters. Garcia was out, however, shortly after daylight, to check on the condition of his horse. With the snow covering even the dried grass, he was quite concerned.

Lolita was standing in a little clearing in the timber when he found her. She appeared calm and relaxed, despite a skiff of snow along her back. The mare was standing, comfortably browsing on the twigs and small branches of the nearby cottonwood trees. Glancing around, Garcia realized that the animal was being quite selective. Ignoring willow, sycamore, and a variety of other shrubs and trees, she was munching happily on the cottonwood.

His two young aspiring horsemen were with him, and immediately grasped the significance of this occurrence. The deer, they informed Heads Off, also use the cottonwood for winter browse. From this time forth, the two youngsters never failed to see that the gray mare had access to plenty of the nourishing browse. Sometimes they cut and carried sticks and bark to the animal, sometimes they led her to the choicest of brushy thickets. Garcia soon realized that he need have no fear for the mare's nutrition. Long Elk and Standing Bird would see to her welfare.

The weeks dragged on, and eventually Garcia, still feeling very much a prisoner of circumstances, began to see hopeful signs. The buds on the willows along the river were beginning to swell. There were tiny shoots of green appearing among the brown dried leaves on the ground under the trees. And one morning he awoke to a clamor of honking in the sky above the camp. He stepped from the lodge to watch, with several other early risers, long lines of calling geese, heading north. Spring must be at hand, he decided. Apparently the People thought the same, because on every face he met was a pleasant smile.

Garcia began to plan his departure. As soon as the prairie grass began to green up, Coyote had told him, the buffalo would return in great numbers. That would be the time to begin his journey. Hunting would be easy, and there would be no need to stop to search for graze or browse for the horse. He began to ride occasionally, to condition Lolita to more demanding activity.

At first he thought that the saddle cinch seemed short because the mare had become a little pot-bellied over the winter. A horse, he knew, feeding on hay or coarse ration, would develop a bulging abdomen, especially when inactive. A hay-belly, his father had always called it.

"Never mind, little lady, we'll soon work that off," he assured the little mare, patting her affectionately.

Lolita did work well, even seemed to enjoy the return to activity in the warming spring sun. But the hay-belly did not seem to recede. In fact, Garcia noted with surprise, the latigo strap seemed even shorter, after one period of a few rainy days' inactivity. He checked again, thinking there might be a twist in the straps. No, everything seemed proper.

"Is something wrong with the elk-dog?" asked

Standing Bird with concern.

The mare stood quietly, apparently comfortable. Garcia checked the animal's general appearance, dreading the discovery of any unsoundness that might prevent his escape. Her coat was still a little rough, shedding in patches as the weather warmed. The ribs were a little prominent, as might be expected at the end of a winter on rough forage. And there remained the prominent abdomen.

Long Elk was squatting on his heels in the character-istic posture of relaxation. Now he pointed beneath the mare's belly, between the back legs.

"Is this wrong, Heads Off?"

Garcia stepped quickly back to stoop for a look. The little mare's udder was enlarging. Mother of God, he thought incredulously, the mare is pregnant!

It was with a considerable mixture of emotion that he considered the situation. The sire would have been the black stallion of the Capitan, he judged, and the prospect intrigued him somewhat. What an excellent breeding! His father would be thrilled, that one of his best Andalusian mares could bear the foal of one of the finest stallions Juan had ever seen.

If, he thought in despair, I am ever able to get out of this cursed country and communicate with my father. The more he thought, the more he realized, this devel-opment would postpone his leaving again. It would be unthinkable to start such a journey on a mount near to foaling. Aside from the inconvenience, if the foaling did not go well, he could easily be alone and on foot in the middle of the wilderness. Impatiently, he realized that it would be several weeks at least, before he could depart.

He attempted to judge just when the mare might deliver. No more than five weeks, his father had always said, after the udder fills. He should have paid more attention to the mares at home. He had no idea when this event had occurred, but thought it must be recent. He tried to calculate with a row of scratches in the mud to represent days, but soon realized he had no clear idea of a date to calculate from. He had lost all track of time, as expressed in the calendar of his own culture. Without being aware of it, he had begun to think in the terms of the People. Behind were the Long Nights Moon, Snow Moon, the Hunger Moon, and the Wakening Moon. This was the Greening Grass Moon, but what month in his culture?

Irritably, he wiped out his scratches in the mud, threw down his stick, and strode back to the lodge. Nothing to do but wait.

After what seemed an interminable number of weeks, Garcia wakened one morning to the soft voice of Long Elk.

"Heads Off! Get up quickly," he whispered excitedly. "There is a small elk-dog!" The youngsters had hardly left the mare unattended for the past weeks. Garcia quickly dressed, and the two raced down the slope to where Standing Bird squatted, pointing proudly.

"It has just come, Heads Off," he reported.

The small, wet shivering creature stood beside the mare's flank, wavering slightly on unsteady legs.

Warm steam rose from the furry black coat, and Lolita gently nuzzled the foal and made soft mothering noises.

Garcia quickly examined the foal. A filly, by God, and a fine one. Long straight legs, good flat bone, a deep chest, and a head like her mother's. The black color at birth meant she'd probably be a gray like her mother when she grew to maturity. He was so exultant over the quality of the foal that he forgot for a time that this creature was the cause of his delayed departure.

This was called forcibly to his attention again by a declaration at tribal council. The People, Hump Ribs announced, would break camp three suns from now, to begin the migration north for the summer. When Garcia heard the news he was furious for a moment. How could they, he fumed, leave him alone and hampered by a week-old foal and a nursing mare?

As reason returned, he realized that Hump Ribs and the People didn't know of his plans. He had been a bit secretive about it for no particular reason, except that, he guessed, he simply didn't trust the savages completely.

The other thing that slowly occurred to him was that, when it got right down to it, the People didn't owe him a thing. He had taken advantage of their hospitality, but aside from a few buffalo kills, hadn't contributed much. Damn, things become complicated, he pondered.

He considered striking out on his own anyway. If the foal couldn't keep up, he could always abandon it or kill it. The mare would suffer the loss only a few days, and would travel better after her milk dried up.

In the end, his horseman's instincts came to the fore. He couldn't do it, he decided. Here was a foal of a quality his father had tried all his life to produce. He could spare a few weeks to allow the filly to grow and gain strength. Then, later in the season, he could start his often-postponed journey. Meanwhile, it seemed, his best possibility was to stay with the People.

༈ 14 ༄

AS THE TRIBE BROKE CAMP and the lodges came down, Coyote and his family had no idea how close they had come to losing their guest. The People straggled over the hill, once again followed by a ludicrous figure. This time, however, the rider wore buckskins and moccasins in addition to chain-mail and body armor. Trotting playfully alongside was a small black elk-dog, and at each flank was a young man of the People.

On the third day of travel, cries of alarm suddenly came from the front of the column. The tribe was straggling along a route over half a mile in length, and was in the middle of a large rolling plain with no shelter. Amid frightened chatter, the People scurried together in one group, children at the center, then women, with warriors at the periphery. Garcia looked in the direction everyone was staring, and saw a similar band of natives on the prairie at a distance of several hundred paces.

Several men stalked forward from the other group, as

Hump Ribs beckoned some of the warriors to join him and stepped forth to meet the strangers. Thoroughly confused, Garcia dismounted and handed his reins to one of the boys, stepping forward to look for Coyote. Coyote saw him coming and beckoned him forward, to join in the second rank of warriors behind Hump Ribs and the sub-chiefs.

"It is the Head Splitters," Coyote explained nervously. "They are enemies of the People. They are fierce fighters."

"Will there be fighting?" Garcia gripped his lance.

"I think not, Heads Off. They will not make trouble, with their women and children nearby. But we must be careful. They are very bad ones."

The strangers now came nearer, haughty and insolent in manner. Several carried bows, but each man had, either dangling from his hand or from his waistband, a long war club. There were a few of these weapons among the People, but Garcia had not seen many. A fist-sized stone, bound or laced tightly to the tip of a slender handle as long as a man's arm. It was easy to see that the weapon was not for the purpose of hunting, but for combat. He began to see the significance of the name "Head Splitters."

"What do they want?" asked the somewhat confused Garcia. Surely they wouldn't fight over a territory as large as the endless prairie, or over possessions. The buffalo, in constant abundance, supplied most of the needs of the nomadic People.

"They like to raid and kill us," answered Coyote. "They are very warlike. They also carry off our children, especially girls. Our women," he confided with a nervous giggle, "are much prettier than theirs."

The two chiefs stopped, facing each other, and to Garcia's surprise, began an apparently friendly conversation. Since much of the dialogue was in sign language, he was able to follow the general flow of ideas. There were the exchange of greetings and small talk about the weather and the buffalo.

"I see you have an elk-dog," said the Head Splitter chief casually, as if he saw elk-dogs every day. Garcia stiffened.

"Oh, yes," replied Hump Ribs just as casually, "it belongs to a friend of the People, who is living with us."

The Head Splitter looked as if he wished more information, but none was offered. The two groups guardedly withdrew, a friendly atmosphere prevailing on the surface. The People suspiciously moved around the other band, and finally resumed the original direction of march. They stayed close together on the trail, however, and sentries were posted at night around the periphery of the camp.

However, no further Head Splitters were seen, and in a few days the People relaxed.

The northward migration continued. Sometimes for a day or two a halt would be called, to hunt or rest. At these brief camp sites, the skin lodges were not used unless the weather became inclement. Brush arbors served for the slight shelter needed, as the mild days and cool comfortable nights continued.

After several weeks' travel, a general air of excitement and anticipation began to be evident among the People. Garcia inquired about it.

"We are only three suns from the gathering place," answered Coyote. "We will meet the other bands of the People."

The excitement of a festival atmosphere rose to a peak a few afternoons later, as the band topped a low range of hills and looked down over a broad expanse of prairie. A meandering slash of darker green trees marked the course of a good-sized stream. Along the near side of this stream were more skin lodges than Garcia had seen in his entire life.

A spontaneous shout arose from the leading elements of Hump Ribs' band, and an answering welcome hail came from the encampment. Hundreds of people moved among the dwellings, and a number of these started forward to greet the newcomers, accompanied by innumerable dogs. Women happily greeted relatives from other bands, and children and young people mingled, chattering and renewing friendships and acquaintances. The happy din and confusion reminded Garcia of the country fairs back home in his childhood.

Hump Ribs led his band to the meadow where an open area had been reserved. Each band, Coyote explained, camped in an assigned area. This was the traditional section in the circle of the encampment, reserved for the Southern band. The same arrangement was true in the council circle, he continued. Each of the chiefs would sit in the corresponding portion of the circle at the Big Council.

Within a short time the pole skeletons of the lodges

were tilting skyward. By the time Sun Boy's torch dipped below the hill in a blaze of crimson and orange and yellow, the People of Hump Ribs' band were at home.

Garcia was, of course, an object of great curiosity to the members of the other bands. At first he was feared and avoided, but very shortly the children, encouraged by their counterparts in Hump Ribs' band, would approach him curiously. Never before had they seen a man with fur upon his face. The openness of their stares bothered the young man considerably.

He was also concerned about his mare and her foal. Members of the other bands were constantly standing and staring at the animals. Garcia had relaxed his anxiety over the past months as to the People's attitude toward the mare. He just wasn't sure about all these strangers. Coyote saw his concern and spoke reassuringly

"They are safe, Heads Off. The camp talk will say that the elk-dogs are the property of our friend. Besides," he giggled, "I think they are constantly watched by your followers Standing Bird and Long Elk."

This did indeed seem true. At all times one or the other of the young men was present, cautioning those who came too close, and haughtily answering the questions of their peers. Garcia finally began to relax.

Toward evening of their first full day in the encampment, Coyote sought out his young guest.

"Heads Off," he announced, "tonight is the Big Council. We will meet in the center of the camp at dark. All the warriors are to come for the meeting."

The young man thought this over. Coyote had casually mentioned this meeting as if he, Garcia, were expected to attend. By Christ's blood, he thought, I'm not one of the "warriors." Still, he felt obliged to go, not only from curiosity, but to make sure nothing occurred that would adversely affect his future plans.

≈ 15 ≈

A FIRE was burning in the center of the clearing as Coyote and Heads Off strolled toward the council. Groups of warriors from the various bands were sitting or squatting in their designated areas, visiting comfortably. Some of the chiefs were already present, seated on robes. The two men found a place beside Mouse Roars in the second rank of warriors, and arranged themselves in the circle.

Hump Ribs strolled forward, spread his robe, and seated himself. Soon the circle was complete. Behind the seated circles of men were a number of women. An even larger number of children and the ever-present dogs moved restlessly around the periphery.

A young man took from a decorated case a long, heavily adorned pipe, and ceremoniously filled it. He handed the instrument to a dignified chief directly across the fire from Hump Ribs, and brought a brand from the fire to light it.

"That one is Many Robes," whispered Coyote. "He is the real-chief of all the People. His is the Northern band."

Many Robes lighted the pipe and ceremoniously blew puffs of smoke to the four directions, and to the earth and the sky. His pipe carrier then handed it to the next chief to the right, and the ceremony was repeated. The chiefs of each band, seven in all, smoked the pipe ceremonially. This was considerably different, Garcia noted, from the "smoke" as a social event in the lodges of friends.

When the pipe had completed the circle, Many Robes ceremoniously knocked the dottle from the bowl, and handed the instrument to his pipe bearer.

"Hear me, my chiefs," he began. "The People are gathered for the Sun Dance. Let each tell how it is with his band."

An aging chief on the west of the circle spoke first.

"I am Black Beaver," he began, "chief of the Mountain band of the People. We have had a good winter. The game was plentiful, and we wintered well. We camped in the Big Timbers, and were not attacked by anyone."

"I am White Bear," related the next chief, "of the Red Rocks band of the People. We have had a hungry winter, but managed to live. Two Suns, one of our warriors, was attacked by a porcupine he was trying to kill to eat, but managed to escape."

A ripple of laughter went round the circle, and even Two Suns managed a wry smile, remembering the painful quills.

Hump Ribs was next in the circle, and the entire group waited expectantly. The fur-bearing stranger and his elk-dog were probably the biggest news in the encampment.

"I am Hump Ribs, chief of the Southern band of the People. We have had a very good winter. Our hunting was helped by our friend Heads Off, who has been living with us since last Ripening Moon. He has the elk-dog which you have all seen.

"We have also seen the Head Splitters," he continued. A murmur came from the circle. This bit of news had been almost eclipsed by the unique quality of the visitor in Hump Ribs' band.

"They had with them their women and children, as we did," Hump Ribs explained, "so there was no fighting."

The greetings continued round the circle, but all news was anticlimax after that of the Southern band.

After each chief's introductory remarks, Many Robes spoke again.

"Tell us, my brothers of the Southern band," he addressed Hump Ribs, "more of your visitor, Heads Off. Where is his tribe?"

Hump Ribs, proud to be the leader of the only band with any real news, warmed to the occasion. He described in detail the incident of their first contact with the stranger. He related the circumstances of the Heads Off name. Everyone chuckled, and Coyote giggled his high-pitched laugh. Heads Off, for the first time, understood the significance of his own name, and chuckled, also. It must have been a spectacular incident to the savages, who had never seen a helmet before.

The real-chief was speaking again. "But let us hear

more of the elk-dog's medicine. How does it help with the hunt?" The connection was still unclear to many in the circle.

Hump Ribs' answer revealed the diplomacy that had made him a chief among the People.

"My chiefs," he protested, "I am not skilled in medicines. Perhaps White Buffalo, our able medicine man, can explain."

Coyote was quietly pleased with the way things were going. It was just as he and Hump Ribs had discussed. Already the Southern band of Hump Ribs was gaining prestige in the council as a result.

White Buffalo shuffled forward. His explanation was simple and straightforward. The newcomer had very strong medicine to control the elk-dog. Basically, this was due to the powerful influence of a device placed in its mouth. This control enabled Heads Off to actually sit and ride upon the animal.

A murmur came from the circle. Apparently many had not yet seen the horse ridden.

So powerful was the medicine, White Buffalo went on, that even two young men of the People had been able to ride upon the elk-dog! More murmurs of astonishment were audible.

Garcia was understanding most of the dialogue and was amused at the reaction of the other bands.

"Now," White Buffalo was continuing, "all this has nothing to do with the buffalo. My medicine brings the buffalo so that Heads Off may ride among them and kill as he wishes with a long spear that he has."

Another murmur, this time of understanding, ran

round the circle. White Buffalo shuffled back to his place.

"My chiefs," Hump Ribs resumed, "it may be that Heads Off will consent to show, for you to see, how his medicine helps with the hunt." He turned and looked over his shoulder at the guest. "Could this be done, Heads Off?"

Garcia nodded, a trifle embarrassed by the situation. No reason why not, he reflected. He could see that Hump Ribs' band was receiving much favorable attention. He could put on a pretty good show for the other chiefs and their followers. It might be interesting. And if the truth were known, the young man was rather enjoying all the personal glory involved.

The time for the great demonstration of elk-dog medicine came a few days later. The scouts had located a small band of buffalo, which seemed to be moving quietly and without alarm. Cautiously, they maneuvered the animals for two days, allowing them time to graze. Finally they were about to enter the selected area, and word went back to the encampment.

A spot had been selected, a flat meadow in a semicircle of hills, forming a sort of amphitheater. The river closed the remaining side of the great natural stage. The entire scenario reminded Garcia of a gigantic rendition of a puppet theater, such as the traveling entertainers and minstrels used in his country.

There were only two narrow exits from the meadow, one at each end where the hills sloped to meet the river. The people were scattered across the hillsides, squatting quietly and remaining perfectly inconspicuous.

The buffalo, led by a wary old cow, entered the arena and moved forward, cropping the lush new grass along the stream. They were beginning to be a bit restless from the quiet harassment of the hunters assigned to move them into the arena. The old cow raised her head, sensing something slightly amiss. She looked around the meadow, and suspected something ominous in the unfamiliar shapes on the hillside. She turned to retreat and found the route blocked by the annoying two-legged creatures that had been following.

At a trot, the cow started for the other exit of the valley, a few hundred paces away. Just at that moment, Garcia rode from behind the shoulder of a low hillock, lowered his lance point, and started his run.

He had selected a fat yearling bull as his quarry. Not only would it provide excellent meat, but the color of this particular animal was a bit out of the ordinary. There was a tendency to variation in color among the creatures, he had noticed, and this was a much lighter animal than most. It was almost a mouse-color, and would serve admirably for the purpose he had in mind.

Garcia had noticed long ago that at the very start of some runs with the lance, there was no doubt as to the outcome. Sometimes it required the utmost in concentration and effort, but occasionally, there was that effortless, perfect run. This was such a run, a perfect demonstration. He knew, when the mare started forward, that the result was preordained.

The lance thrust home, directly in front of the hill where the chiefs of the council sat. The buffalo slowed, and as Garcia reined the horse and withdrew the weapon, the bull stumbled and fell. Its companions galloped clumsily on, disappearing around the bend of the river.

Garcia rode slowly toward the group of chiefs on the hillside. He reined the horse, and ceremoniously dipped the bloodied lance point downward and up again.

"I give this kill," he announced in a ringing voice, "to Many Robes, chief of the People!"

❧ 16 ❧

M UCH OF THE SIGNIFICANCE of the week-long Sun Dance was lost on Garcia. He simply was not interested enough in the event to pay attention. He did loaf around the big brush arbor and watch the dancers from time to time. Coyote answered his occasional questions, glad for any interest the guest showed.

The young man assumed, and correctly, that part of the function of the Sun Dance was social. It was apparently the one yearly occasion in which the entire scattered tribe of the People came together for a time. Friendships and acquaintances were renewed, and relatives could catch up on family news.

Of course, Garcia saw that a major theme of the festival was that of the buffalo. An effigy of a large bull had been fashioned from cedar brush and placed in the arbor. The skin of an actual animal, with head still attached, completed the caricature.

Garcia was a bit puzzled as to why it was the "Sun"

Dance. The connection somehow eluded him. Coyote's answer was brief and to the point.

"Sun Boy's torch nearly goes out in the Long Nights Moon. But now he has a new brighter torch and the heat makes the grass grow, so the buffalo return."

After all the dances were danced, ceremonies held, songs sung, and sacrifices offered, the Sun Dance ultimately came to an end. By the time the various bands had begun to scatter in various directions for the season, Garcia had made an observation. There was a good reason why the entire People could not stay together. So large a group would find it difficult to find the necessary game to furnish the required volume of food. A problem existed here, he realized. A band such as that of Hump Ribs must be large enough for mutual defense, but not large enough to frighten the herds and make hunting difficult.

Still, it seemed that a strong band was a desirable thing. This became apparent when Hump Ribs' People struck camp to travel to the east, where White Buffalo declared the herds to be. The old medicine man was usually correct, Garcia noted with amusement. He had a feeling that perhaps this was true because there were buffalo almost everywhere. If the band found large numbers of the animals, White Buffalo was quick to take credit. If not, the old man had a tendency to blame interfering factors that were disturbing his medicine. A very clever man, Garcia decided.

The young man was walking beside Coyote, resting from the saddle. He had allowed Long Elk to ride the mare for the present. Mouse Roars approached, and fell in beside the two men. He appeared pleased.

"We have gained seven lodges," he announced proudly. "Maybe ten warriors. Of course some are just curious, but there are some good fighting men. Two Pines of the Red Rocks band has brought his own lodge and that of his daughter's husband."

It was a lengthy speech for the quiet man. Garcia glanced up and down the straggling column. The group was indeed larger. He was puzzled.

"That was a good thing, Heads Off, to give the kill to the real-chief," Mouse Roars continued. "You have been good in his eyes."

Garcia was still confused about the new lodges in the group. Apparently a family could transfer allegiance from one band to another.

"Oh, yes," answered Coyote in answer to the question. "They go with whatever chief seems to have the strongest medicine this year. Some men change every year. We do not need that sort, but we have gained some very good men, too. They think the elk-dog medicine is strong. And, of course, the Red Rocks were hungry last winter. They look for a stronger chief."

Both Coyote and Mouse Roars seemed extremely pleased that the shifting weight of political prestige has favored Hump Ribs' Southern band.

During the days of the somewhat leisurely march, Garcia began to work with the training of Lolita's foal. From the time of its birth, the two youngsters had handled, petted, and groomed, until the animal was quite familiar with the human touch. Garcia had fashioned a sort of halter from strips of buckskin, but he realized that equipment would be a problem. At home in his father's stable there were always plenty of ropes, bridles, and assorted items for use in the training process. He wished he had paid a little more attention. Like a lot of other things, he reflected gloomily, that he hadn't appreciated until they were absent. Well, no matter, he'd be out of this in a few weeks. By the time the People moved south for the winter, he intended to have the foal well broken to tie or to lead. Then he could start his journey to his own people, well equipped and able to travel.

One of his most direct needs was for a rope. He had the light lariat on his saddle, used for picketing his horse. However, it could not be used for both animals. Besides, he noticed its strands becoming frayed. Eventually it must wear out.

He examined the plaited strands. Maybe he could twist strips of skin like that. Cautiously, he cut the knot from the end of the rope, saving it to study in case he had trouble trying to retie the loose ends later. Several times he unwound a few inches of rope and replaited carefully. By trial and error he managed to fairly well duplicate the original plait. Pleased, he secured the end with a new knot and went to ask Big Footed Woman about some thongs for a new rope.

As soon as the new lariat began to take shape, Garcia's two young imitators grasped the principles involved and had to try their hands, also. Standing Bird, especially, proved to have nimble fingers, and his plaited lariat soon grew faster than either of the others.

Garcia was still concerned about a method for control of the animal. Horses were easily controlled by means of the bit in the mouth, but he had only one bit. It was needed for the mare. He had long since realized that the People had no knowledge of metals whatever. Perhaps he'd just wait until he arrived back in civilization.

It was Coyote who produced a solution. He pointed to the ring of the bit. "The elk-dog cannot escape the circle, where the medicine is, and must do as you wish. Maybe the circle could be made of a rope."

Scornful at first, Garcia thought about it. He was learning to respect the opinions of Coyote. Maybe it would be worth a try.

He decided to experiment with the mare, since she was already easily handled. Placing a length of slender rope through her mouth, he brought the ends under and tied a knot beneath the animal's chin. Another turn on the knot served to keep the circle from tightening, and the two long dangling ends became reins. Lolita rolled her tongue over the unfamiliar object in her mouth, but when Garcia vaulted onto her back, responded well. With a little practice, the animal seemed as easily controlled as with the iron bit.

The foal, now growing rapidly, was introduced to the rawhide version of elk-dog medicine. Soon, to the delight of the boys, Garcia could drive her from the ground, walking behind or to the side. He cautioned them that the small elk-dog would not be strong enough to sit on for many moons. The next time the band moved, however, he was able to place small articles of baggage on her back, tied to a strap around her body.

Carrying a light weight would accustom her to objects on her back. Then, when she was mature enough to be ridden, the filly would already understand the entire process. Garcia was pleased. Perhaps he could ultimately show his father a well-trained animal.

He was beginning to look forward now to the journey south. He could even use the young filly to carry some of his lighter supplies. It seemed that Hump Ribs would never call for the annual migration to begin, but eventually he did.

The first chilly nights of autumn were beginning to be felt as the band moved into the general area of the previous winter camp. Supplies were being stored for the winter, and hunting was good. Garcia had not yet revealed his intention to leave. He wasn't sure why, but he rather dreaded the announcement of his plans.

I'll tell them tonight, he finally decided, after this one more day of hunting. His lance had accounted for many buffalo, and the People would have another fat year.

Garcia had no premonition, as he started on one last day with the hunters of the People. That fateful day would not only prevent his departure once more, but alter the course of his life as much as any other single event.

17

T HE DAY began like any other pleasant day in the Ripening Moon. The weather was crisp, but the sun was warm, and the hunt successful.

A group of a dozen or more buffalo were located, and the hunters maneuvered into a favorable position and concealed themselves in the tall prairie grass. Heads Off then circled with the elk-dog, and approached the herd from the opposite side. When he started his charge with the lance, the animals fled, as had been expected, directly toward the hidden hunters. Three more buffalo were taken.

Garcia noticed that the rest of the herd did not retreat very far. They were grazing quietly just beyond the hill. Maybe, he thought, it might be possible to make another run. He remounted and nudged the mare forward.

It was a bit more difficult, because the buffalo had been recently frightened and were now skittish. It took him longer to overtake the running animals. When his lance finally thrust home, it was at an inopportune moment. The buffalo were charging up a rocky slope, and it was apparent that the chase must end directly. Garcia, however, was determined to make one last kill, and made his strike from an unusual angle, just as the fleeing animal swerved.

The lance thrust true, but he felt the point strike bone, and then felt, rather than heard, a sharp snap. Dreading what he knew he would see, he withdrew the weapon to examine the point. His worst fears were realized as he saw the steel blade broken cleanly near the shaft. At least a hand's span of the pointed tip was missing.

Quickly Garcia dismounted, and ran to the dying bull. He soon realized the futility of any action, and sat impatiently on a rock to wait for the women of the butchering party. They were quite sympathetic when they arrive and promised to retrieve the point of the real-spear from the carcass. Garcia sat, frustrated and fuming with anger at his own carelessness.

At last, one of the old women gave a cry of delight and held aloft in a bloody fist the missing point. A wide toothless smile spread across her lined face as she offered the object to Heads Off. The young man, pre-occupied with the gravity of the situation, barely thanked her as he snatched the point and stepped into the saddle to return to camp.

Cursed luck, he fumed silently as he rode. Here he was, in the midst of the wilderness, without weapons, except for his short belt knife. Not only did this turn of events prevent his obtaining fresh meat, but it had ren-dered him completely defenseless. Until he could repair the broken lance, there was no possibility of his leaving to return to his people.

The mending of the lance point seemed not too com-plicated, Garcia thought. It was more of a nuisance than a serious problem. He had seen the armorers fashion such weapons, and the process had seemed simple in their brawny hands. He would simply heat the broken parts and hammer the hot metal back together. He must have the proper equipment, how-ever, even though makeshift. A large boulder of the hard red variety would serve as an anvil. A smaller stone, polished round by centuries in the stream, would function as a smith's hammer. He selected his anvil and quickly built a fire next to it. Coyote squatted nearby, fascinated by the procedure.

On the first few attempts, the broken steel failed to become even red hot. Garcia knew that the weld would require an intense white heat. Dejected, he sat down and thought the matter over. The two main ingredients he lacked were charcoal and a bellows, he decided.

Charcoal, he believed, could be made without much trouble. He piled hardwood sticks on his fire, and while it progressed to a thick bed of glowing coals, tried to think about how he could possibly construct a bellows. Puzzled, Coyote watched the young man douse water on his fire, sort out the damp chunks of charcoal, and spread them carefully aside to dry. Surely, he pondered, Heads Off has now gone mad over the loss of his real-spear.

By sundown, however, Garcia had assembled quite a supply of the fuel. Reluctantly, he discontinued the process for the night, still puzzling over how he might construct a bellows. Coyote's family remained quiet and aloof, somewhat fearful of the smoldering temper of their guest.

If there were only a way, he pondered, to make a leather bag spurt a stream of air into the fire. His wandering glance fell on the waterskin hanging over his bed. Coyote now became certain that Heads Off was completely mad, as the young man leaped to his feet with a cry of joy. The children cowered in the farthest reaches of the lodge and watched Heads Off draw the belt knife and start to cut a hole in his perfectly good waterskin.

The madness seemed to take a definite direction, however. With other scraps of leather and thongs,

Heads Off was apparently trying to make something. Once he took a torch and went out into the dogwood thicket behind the lodges. Coyote felt obliged to accompany him to protect him from his own madness. The little warrior even held the torch while his guest cut and trimmed an armful of the tough, flexible sticks.

Back in the lodge again, Garcia began to construct a frame for his bellows. Clumsy looking by any standards, the paddle-shaped halves of woven sticks were hinged at one end with thongs, and the altered water-skin was tied between the flat surfaces. After a bit of adjustment and experimenting, he moved closer to the fire and pointed the spout of the flask into the hot coals. Experimentally, he pumped the stick handles.

The result was most gratifying. Ashes flew, and sparks scattered over the floor, alarming the children for a moment, and producing a torrent of protest from Big Footed Woman. More importantly, the dull red of the coals instantly responded with a hot glow. Exultant, Garcia sat and played with the device, quickly learning to pump slowly for a constant, even heat. Coyote was greatly relieved that the madness did indeed have some purpose. For some reason, Heads Off needed a hotter fire. If this device would accomplish that purpose, very good. True, it seemed simpler to merely blow on it, but this was medicine that had to do with the real-spear. Maybe he would understand the medicine when he saw Heads Off use it.

Next morning, Garcia could hardly wait to try his luck at the repair. The two men went to the makeshift smithy, and Garcia kindled his fire. When the charcoal began to glow, he cautiously began use of the skin bellows. The red glow brightened, and the bed of coals became hotter, progressing toward white heat. He turned to place the broken spear in the coals, losing some heat as he stopped the rhythmic pumping. Instantly Coyote was at his side, taking the bellows and resuming the pumping of air.

It's going to work, Garcia exulted to himself. By Christ, it's going to work! The steel became dull red, then cherry colored, and finally an intense glowing white. Quickly he removed the parts from the fire and laid them upon the stone anvil. He motioned to Coyote to hold the spear shaft, and holding the other portion with a piece of leather, began to pound with his stone. It was necessary to reheat twice, but finally he was satisfied that the weld was solid. He removed the spear from the anvil, and thrust the weapon into the water of the stream, as he had seen the armorers do with a barrel of water.

There was a loud hiss and a metallic pop, and the lance came from the water with the point missing again. The sudden cooling had cracked the weld. Garcia was thrust into the depths of despair. He fumbled around in the shallow water and finally came up with the broken point.

How did the armorers do it? Could it be that they had allowed the weapon to partially cool before the quenching? He couldn't remember.

Three more times he tried in the coming days, and each time the weld failed to hold. Once it remained firm even after the quenching, and for a moment he was exultant. But then, as he tapped the lance experimentally on the ground, it snapped again. It was no use. Dejected, he sat on the ground, idly picking at the grass. He was again a prisoner of circumstances, and here loomed again the necessity of another winter in the company of the savages. Maybe even longer, he thought gloomily.

Just then, one of the other men of the band approached. Garcia recognized Stone Breaker, an older man with a bad limp. Too incapacitated to hunt, this man was considered expert in the chipping of flints to make arrowheads. Garcia had noticed men proudly showing their weapons made by the Stone Breaker. The man approached hesitantly and extended his hand.

"Heads Off," he began, "I have made a new point for the real-spear."

On his palm lay a long, slender spear point, of the finest of blue-gray stone. Coyote, looking at the weapon, thought he had never seen such a splendid example of Stone Breaker's art. It must have taken many hours' patient work.

Garcia looked at the gracefully shaped point, and was suddenly overcome with the weeks and months of frustration. He seized the object, and in a sudden rage, flung it from him as far as he could. The last damned insult! He strode away, furious, to be alone, while Coyote and Stone Breaker stood, puzzled and disappointed.

Stupid, ignorant savages, he muttered to himself. Thinking they could replace a fine blade of Toledo steel with a chunk knocked off a cursed rock!

Damn them all, anyway. He was out of sight of the camp now, and stopped to sit and rest. A slight irritation called his attention to his right forefinger. Blood oozed from a clean-edged gash, apparently made when he threw the spear head.

Mother of God, he mused. The damned thing was certainly sharp! I'll have to grant them that.

ᘓ 18 ᘔ

IN THE DAYS FOLLOWING GARCIA'S FIT OF TEMPER, he spent much time alone. He seemed to lose interest in the horses and nearly stopped communicating with the children of the lodge and with others of the People. Even Coyote was unable to draw him into conversation.

Coyote understood why. The loss of the real-spear, and the inability of Heads Off to fix it. He guessed further that this made the young man feel defenseless. The clever little warrior even had some inkling that Heads Off desired to depart for his own country. This, of course, he could not do without weapons.

But there was a more important consideration. By means of the skills of Heads Off, the People had fared well in the past year. Many buffalo had been killed. The children were fat and the women happy. Every lodge had many robes and skins, and the supplies for winter were in plenty.

Something must be done to restore the hunting ability of Heads Off, as well as his disposition. Heads Off was becoming very unpleasant to be around. After long consideration, Coyote came to a decision. Stone Breaker must try again. Perhaps he and Coyote together could persuade Heads Off to try the new weapon.

Stone Breaker was not enthusiastic about the project. He still smarted from the bitterness of rejection, but eventually Coyote's enthusiasm prevailed. They could, he insisted, fashion a real-spear balanced like the broken one. It would have to be longer than the spears of the People. He, Coyote, would measure the necessary length. The point for the real-spear had been retrieved, fortunately undamaged. It could be bound to the shaft tightly with rawhide, applied wet. Shrinkage in drying would make the weapon as solid as a single piece. The slightly longer flint point could be supported by carefully scraped projections of the spear shaft, fitted closely along the flat sides. Then they could show Heads Off the finished product.

It was difficult not to become interested in Coyote's enthusiastic descriptions. Soon he and Stone Breaker were working on the shaft of the weapon, scraping and polishing and trying for fit and for balance.

When the real-spear was finally ready, Stone Breaker refused to have anything to do with its presentation. He had tasted the angry temper of Heads Off, and wanted no more. Coyote was perhaps a little more dubious than he cared to admit. He decided to wait until the time was right.

The opportunity came a few days later. A herd of bison, shaggy in winter hair, drifted near the camp of the People. They could be plainly seen on the distant hillside. Coyote stopped by the lodge of Stone Breaker to pick up the real-spear, and then approached Heads Off, not quite as confident as he pretended.

"Heads Off," he began firmly, "there are buffalo on the hills. Before you become angry again, I ask you to try this real-spear. It can do no worse than to fail to work." He held the weapon forward.

Garcia hesitated, anger flaring. Well, why not look at the damned thing, he finally decided. He snatched the slender shaft and hefted it in his hand. To his surprise, the balance was good. He'd certainly used weapons with less balance. He examined the point, ruefully remembering his sore finger. Well, why not? He'd give it a try. He went to saddle the mare.

The hunt was highly successful. The horse worked well, and the quarry ran straight away, providing an excellent target. And the lance worked well, he had to admit. There was a slightly different sensation at the moment of penetration, but the weapon was certainly efficient. Garcia examined the blade again. If anything, the slightly saw-toothed flint might be even more efficient than the smooth edge, he thought. It might easily cause more internal damage and bleeding. His spirits began to rise. Perhaps this cursed rock would be the answer to his problems.

His good humor restored again, Garcia presented the kill to Stone Breaker as an apology. He became almost as euphoric as he had been depressed before. He would find himself chuckling aloud at the thoughts of the tales he could tell his friends when he returned to civilization. They probably thought him dead. How amazed they would be to learn that he had lived among the savages, and had actually killed buffalo with a stone-tipped spear! He looked forward with even more eagerness to the end of the winter, when travel would become possible.

The family of Coyote was certainly grateful for the return of the easy-going good humor of their guest. His interest in his surroundings returned, and once more even the smaller children engaged him in conversation.

One event of interest that fall was the traditional Warriors' Dance of the People. Garcia supposed that it had been held the previous year, but he didn't remember it. He recalled that at the time he had just begun to learn the language. He had, in fact, still regarded the People as little above the animal level.

This dance, Coyote explained, was a sort of remembrance of past deeds of valor. The songs, sung to the monotonous beat of the drum, were stories of the past. One recounted the tale of a battle with the Head Splitters, and of a brave warrior of the People who stood alone until help came. Another was a story of three warriors who fought a real-cat, a puma, in hand-to-hand combat.

Interspersed were dances that honored the living warriors now present. All the warriors, in their best clothing and headdresses, danced in the open dance ground, while the women watched and sometimes kept rhythm with clapping hands.

Suddenly a woman, the wife of Mouse Roars, walked into the arena and laid at his feet a beautifully tanned robe. Mouse Roars stopped, thrust his spear into the ground beside the robe, and stood, arms folded. The other dancers and the drum stopped.

"What's happening?" whispered Garcia to Tall One. "I don't understand."

"She honors him. He must stand there until someone accepts the gift and so honors him."

Garcia nodded, not understanding at all. Presently a ragged little woman crept into the circle and picked up the robe, nodding to Mouse Roars. He nodded in return, and the dance resumed.

Later the puzzled young man asked Coyote about it.

"Yes," explained Coyote. "A warrior's family can show how proud they are of him this way. The person who takes the gift says, 'Yes, I think so, too!' Besides," he continued, "this is a good way to help the poorer people. You saw the woman who took Mouse Roars' gift. She has no husband, and is very poor. It honors Mouse Roars to be able to help her."

This entire custom was so very foreign to Garcia's culture that he found it quite hard to understand. He did grasp the idea, though, that it accomplished the honoring of a loved one and a gift to the poor. And these are the people, he thought in amazement, that I thought had no social customs.

Garcia's interest and concern with his horses had also returned. He and his young followers had an easy time caring for the animals in the mild, open winter that followed. The grass began to grow early in the Greening Moon, and the impatient Garcia began to condition the horses with long rides. This time, he vowed, when the People move north, this time there's nothing to stop me. I move south!

These pleasant thoughts were on his mind one balmy afternoon as he groomed the mare after a good workout. He was on a grassy hill just across the river from the encampment, and paused to look over the tops of the lodges. Smoke from cooking fires snaked lazily upward from the apex of each dwelling, and all seemed well with the world.

Motion in the distance, beyond the village, caught his eye. Buffalo running? He shaded his eyes with his hand and studied the moving figures. No, by Christ, horses! Moving at an easy canter, and coming this way. His people had come for him! Leaving the mare to graze, he started down the hill toward the camp.

The horsemen were drawing rapidly nearer, and suddenly doubts assailed his mind. He stopped for a better look. Ten, maybe twelve men. And they're not wearing armor. That's what had appeared inconsistent. Then what—Mother of God, the realization finally sank home as a chill crawled up the back of his neck and made his hair prickle.

Mother of God, those aren't my people, they're savages! Savages, on horseback, and we're being attacked!

At almost the same instant, he heard screams and shouts from among the lodges, and women and children started to run toward the river.

"Run, run," a woman screamed. "The Head Splitters!"

ᘒ 19 ᘒ

G ARCIA broke into a run toward the lodges. People were clattering and splashing across the river at the gravel bar, running past him into the broken area behind to try to hide in the rocks and timber.

He saw the riders sweep down toward the first of the lodges. An old man, Black Dog, Garcia believed he was called, stepped proudly forward to meet the invaders, bow in hand. Even above the shouts and screams could be heard Black Dog's high-pitched quavering voice in the death song.

"The grass and the sky go on forever,
But today is a good day to die!"

The old warrior managed to loose one or two arrows before he was trampled under the hooves of the horses.

Garcia tried to evaluate the situation as he ran. The invaders didn't sit their horses well, he noticed. Sitting too far back, bouncing around a lot. Pretty unfamiliar with horses. There was one exception. A tall, muscular chief in the lead was mounted on a superb stallion. White with blood-red spots over the entire body, this animal was the type Garcia had heard referred to at home as a "tiger horse." Undoubtedly such a horse had belonged to a man of high rank. Probably the savages had stolen it and the other animals from one of the Spanish colonies to the west. He was sure there were colonies in that area. Perhaps the Head Splitter had learned to ride there. Or maybe he just had a natural instinct for handling a horse. No matter now, Garcia thought numbly as he clattered across the gravel bar and sprinted toward Coyote's lodge.

A chance thought flitted across his mind as he dashed inside to grab his lance. A half-forgotten thought from another world.

"When engaging in combat," the instructor at the academy had stated, "it may be very useful to try first to kill one or more of the officers or leaders of the enemy."

Garcia dashed among the lodges, looking for the tall chief on the tiger horse. People rushed back and forth in apparently aimless fashion, complete confusion reigning. There seemed to be very little resistance, and the horsemen were taking utmost advantage of the chaos. Although not the best riders, they had apparently counted heavily on the shock effect. The People had never before in all their history been attacked by mounted warriors. Reaction to this hitherto unknown threat was one of sheer unreasoning panic.

Garcia saw an old woman shuffle feebly into an open area, then turn in confusion. She took a few steps toward the river, then hesitated, turned and started back to her lodge, then reversed again. A horseman swept past and she tumbled into the dust, limp as a rag doll. He couldn't be sure whether she had been struck by the war club or by a flying hoof.

A little girl, clutching a doll in her arms, stood screaming hysterically in front of a lodge, looking for her parents. Her answer came not from the People, but from an enemy horseman. The child was seized from behind by one arm, and thrown forcibly across the horse like a piece of baggage. Her doll fell unnoticed as she continued to kick and scream. That's it, thought Garcia, too far away to help. Fight him! Give them all the trouble you can!

Here and there, a warrior made a lone stand with bow or spear. These efforts seemed mostly ineffective. The mobility of the horsemen and the lack of any organized defense was taking a toll. Garcia saw one man take a stand, then break and run in terror as a horseman thundered down on him. He fell, only a few paces beyond his discarded weapons.

"Stand and fight!" Garcia found himself yelling. The excitement raced through his blood, causing his heart to pound and his ears to roar. With the height of battle came also frustration. He had not been able to strike a single blow in the defense. Fleeing people still ran past him, heading for the river. He ran among the lodges, trying to find where the focus of the conflict might be. The effort seemed useless. The entire battle was a series of isolated, unrelated events, each of which, it appeared, was to the disadvantage of the People. Garcia began to fear the complete annihilation of the band as he saw another warrior fall.

It was almost a relief to see a savage on a big raw-boned bay take notice of him and start a charge. The rider thundered down on him, swinging a war club. He readied the lance and braced himself for the impact.

From the corner of his eye, the young man saw

Mouse Roars step around his lodge, as calmly as if he were going for a stroll. The warrior fitted an arrow to his bowstring and dropped to one knee, loosing the bolt at Garcia's assailant in one smooth motion. The man somersaulted over the back of the horse as if swatted by a giant hand, and the riderless animal brushed past and splashed across the river to escape the melee.

Garcia glanced around at Mouse Roars, who had just dropped his eyes to fit another arrow. Around the lodge stepped the tiger horse, directly behind the warrior. The Head Splitter was only a few paces away, completely unseen by his intended victim. Before Garcia's shouted warning could be heard, the young chief swung his heavy stone club. Mouse Roars slumped forward, his weapon under him.

With a cry of agony, the wife of Mouse Roars rushed from the lodge and flung herself protectively across his body. The chief on the spotted horse circled, stepping daintily around the sobbing woman. Then, he apparently decided she was not young enough or attractive enough to abduct. The great bloody stone swung again.

Garcia screamed a challenge and dashed toward the enemy, readying his lance. For the first time the Head Splitter chief seemed to notice him. He kicked the horse forward in a charge, the heavy club swinging in a whistling circle as he gained momentum.

At the last moment, as he looked directly into his victim's face, the young chief checked his horse momentarily. In retrospect, Garcia decided that the unexpected sight of a bearded face may have caused a moment's hesitation. That moment, a slight check in the smooth rhythm of the horse and the swing of the club, was the deciding factor. Ducking under the arc of the club, Garcia thrust the lance forward with all his strength. The razor-sharp flint passed closely along the right side of the horse's neck and found the bare unprotected midriff of the Head Splitter.

Garcia grasped a dangling rein, stumbled, and fell. The frightened stallion reared and plunged, trying to rid himself of the horrible, flopping bloody thing on his back. The leather rein burned through Garcia's fingers, stopped only by a knot near the end. The dying Head Splitter fell to the ground, and at last the horse stopped fighting.

"Catch the elk-dogs," shouted Garcia, seeing another loose animal.

The invaders were retreating, but in an orderly fashion. It could be seen that across some of the horses' withers, the riders held kicking and screaming children. Lamenting wails of mourning began to arise in the camp as family members were discovered dead or missing. People began to straggle back across the river. Young Standing Bird stood numbly, staring at the bodies of his parents in front of the lodge.

Long Elk assisted in catching and picketing the loose horses. The big bay gelding had joined Lolita and her yearling filly across the river. There was another mare, an attractive chestnut, wandering loose among the lodges, and the big tiger horse. Garcia and Long Elk returned to find a hastily called council in session.

According to present information, three of the enemy

were dead. One had been struck by the first arrow of the brave old warrior, Black Dog. There was the horseman killed by Mouse Roars, and the young chief on the tiger horse, killed by the real-spear of Heads Off.

Seven of the People were dead, and one woman badly injured. In addition, four were missing. Three girls or young women and one boy of ten summers, it was said.

Their names were related, and anyone knowing their whereabouts was asked to speak. Silence. A cold fear began to close around the throat of Garcia. One of the missing, presumed abducted, was Tall One, daughter of Coyote.

ᘰ 20 ᘳ

DISCUSSION followed as to what should be done. Move rapidly north, said one sub-chief, and join the rest of the People. No, countered another, move east, out of the usual range of the Head Splitters. Still another faction wanted to move northwest into the mountains to hide.

The astonished Garcia realized that the main thrust of these arguments was somehow wrong. All consideration was being given to running and hiding, none to fighting or defense. He stood the argument as long as he could, then shouted into the discussion.

"Jesus Christ," he screamed at them, "the bastards have killed your people and stolen your women! Isn't anybody going after them?"

He glanced around the now quiet circle, at the surprised faces. Suddenly he realized that he had been shouting at them in Spanish. They had not understood one word. Forcing calmness, he began again, addressing the chief, Hump Ribs.

"My chief," he said, carefully holding himself in check, "the Head Splitters are no more than this many." He held his ten fingers before him. "Their chief is dead. We can follow and recover our children." A catch in his voice revealed that perhaps this was more important to him than even he realized. "Perhaps we could even get more of their elk-dogs. I am ready to go and try this."

"I go with you, Heads Off," spoke a voice behind him, the orphaned Standing Bird, now the head of his father's lodge.

"And I," spoke Long Elk.

Hump Ribs was surprised, but not so much as to lose his composure. He recognized a potential threat to his prestige, yet saw possibilities in this turn of events. He held up his hand, and the murmuring circle grew quiet.

"Wait," he said majestically. "If there is to be a war party, I will lead it"—a ripple of approval spread— "with the help of Heads Off." The ripple became an optimistic mutter.

Plans were quickly made, and by the time darkness fell, the war party of fifteen was on the trail. The general direction was plain, and tracking of a group of horses easy in the light of a three-quarter moon. Apparently no effort was being made to cover the trail. The Head Splitters' war parties were not accustomed to being followed. One dead horse was found, an arrow jutting from its flank. The arrow was identified as that of Black Dog. His second shot, too, had been effective.

The general direction of the march was southward. Garcia, with his military training, was sharply aware of direction. It would be invaluable in case of unforeseen circumstances or separation from the group. He kept his bearings by watching the constellation of Ursa Major as it wheeled around the pole star.

Coyote sat beside him as they paused for a short rest stop. The little warrior noticed his studying of the sky.

"Those are the Seven Hunters, Heads Off," he volunteered. "They point the way to the real-star, which is always in the same place. Their lodge is there."

Garcia nodded. "We call it the Great Bear." He had ceased to be surprised at new information about the People's beliefs. "My people think it looks like a big bear with a long tail."

Coyote giggled, and they spent the next few moments pointing at the constellation, and discussing its appearance. "It looks more like a skunk than a bear," ventured Coyote.

Kookooskoos, the great owl, called from a nearby wooded ravine, and his mate answered from farther up the stream. The shadowy figures of buffalo moved across the moonlight of the hillside. Except for the extreme importance of the mission, the night would have been one for pure enjoyment.

The advance scout returned to report no sign of the war party ahead, but that the trail was still plain. From the sign, he counted no more than a dozen of the enemy. Apparently it was a small, fast-moving mounted party, depending on surprise hit-and-run tactics. Very well, thought Garcia. Both sides can play the surprise game.

Some time after midnight, word passed back down the column. The night camp of the Head Splitters was ahead, said the advance scouts. The group gathered to plan the attack.

"The prisoners are on the far side beyond the fire. I think they are tied," said the scout. "There is one sentry, over near the place where the elk-dogs are."

"My chief," Garcia suggested, "I would take Long Elk and Standing Bird. We can steal the elk-dogs," he indicated the coils of rope over his shoulder, "while someone cuts the prisoners loose. Who is the best bowman?"

All eyes turned to a quiet young man in the second row of warriors.

"Can you put the sentry down for me without a noise?"

"I think so, Heads Off." The other warriors nodded.

"He can do it," agreed Hump Ribs. "What do you plan?"

"Let whoever is the best stalker go around to release the prisoners. When he hears the horses move out, he and the girls can escape in the confusion."

"It is a good plan." The chief nodded. "The rest will creep up close and attack if the elk-dog men are discovered. Let us all meet afterward under that cut-in-two hill beneath the tree." He pointed to a distant lone tree.

The sentry was either very inexperienced or overly confident. He stood upright, clearly visible in the moonlight, and made only a soft gurgle as the arrow found his throat and he sank to the ground. Garcia and his young horsemen moved swiftly among the animals, knotting the ropes around lower jaws. He selected mounts for each to ride, and they vaulted to the horses' backs, holding the lead ropes of the others. So far there had been no alarm, but now there was a stirring in the enemy camp. Fearful for the prisoners, Garcia gave a long yell and kicked his horse into a canter.

The sleeping warriors sprang up and were briefly silhouetted against the sky, targets for the bowmen of Hump Ribs' group. Confusion reigned in the camp. It was doubtful whether any of the Head Splitters managed even one shot before the skirmish was over.

The People quietly withdrew, leaving an undetermined number of enemy dead and wounded. Some favored returning to finish the job, but Hump Ribs dissuaded them.

"Let them return to their tribe," he said generously. "Let them tell how they were defeated by the People."

The entire party regathered under the big lone tree, and all were accounted for. The erstwhile prisoners were happily restored to the group, and the journey back to the village began. Garcia leaned down and helped the Tall One up behind him on the horse, in a big-brotherly way. However, it was not a sisterly way at all in which she wrapped long arms around his waist. And by the time they journeyed even part way home, Garcia had been forced into some very serious thinking.

He had seen the look in the eyes of the Tall One as the moonlight struck her face when he lifted her to the horse. A look of pure, devoted adoration. And he had come to a decision. He had to have this woman.

❧ 21 ☙

EARLY NEXT MORNING Garcia approached the girl's father. He had decided to follow strictly the customs of the People. He would be expected to offer something of value, but had very little of material worth.

"Coyote," he began hesitantly. "I would like to speak with you."

Coyote nodded, waiting.

"I—I wish to marry your daughter, the Tall One," he blurted. "I would offer you the small elk-dog."

Coyote was delighted, but managed to conceal his pleasure, and appeared to be deliberating.

"Heads Off," he pondered, "I suppose this would be a good thing, but I have no use for a small elk-dog." The young man's disappointment became obvious.

"Perhaps my son, Long Elk, could help me with it," Coyote continued. "Yes, I think it is good. It can take place in the Moon of Falling Leaves. The women will start to make a lodge worthy of a warrior of the People."

Garcia would have liked to protest that he couldn't wait until the Moon of Falling Leaves, but decided to forego that comment. He had considerably mixed feelings about the interview as he wandered out of the lodge. It had been somewhat easier than he'd thought, obtaining Coyote's consent. But he'd had something much more immediate in mind. Like tonight, perhaps. Still, he could see the advantages of having their own lodge. He had wondered how a nuptial night might be possible in the close quarters of her parents' lodge. Completely forgotten was the fact that a few hours earlier he had been entirely ready to leave the People for good.

He wandered among the lodges, confused by the rapid events of the past day. A constant high-pitched mourning song came from various areas of the village, as families of the dead prepared for the burial ritual. In the timber along the stream, scaffolds were being prepared to receive the bodies.

In front of the lodge of Mouse Roars, the warrior's second wife knelt beside two robe-wrapped figures. She had gashed her forearms and upper chest in mourning, and rocked slowly back and forth as she wailed her lament. Young Standing Bird stood nearby with arms folded, stoic in his grief.

Garcia was deeply touched. He had grown to respect and admire Mouse Roars for his ability with weapons. In addition, the warrior had always been modest about his skills. A man whose deeds spoke louder than his words deserved respect. Also, Garcia felt close to young Standing Bird. He felt that the youth showed great promise as a horseman.

"I am sorry, my friend," he spoke clumsily. "Your father was a great warrior. He saved my life."

Standing Bird nodded solemnly. "Mouse Roars spoke well of you, also, Heads Off. He said I could learn much from you."

Later, Garcia assisted in the transporting of the wrapped bodies to the burial scaffolds. The favorite bow of Mouse Roars was ceremonially broken and placed with his body for use in the hereafter.

Returning to the village, the young man encountered Long Elk.

"Heads Off," began the youth, "will you come and tell us about the elk-dogs?" Garcia had nearly forgotten the captured horses.

They crossed the river and found that a small cluster of people were gathered to admire the animals. Several youngsters were cautiously moving among the horses, experimentally touching and handling. He realized with a pang of regret that these were the boys of the Rabbit Society, now leaderless because of the death of Mouse Roars. Several slightly older youths, young men of the Hunter Society, were also present.

"Will you show us how to use them?" asked Long Elk.

Garcia nodded, and examined each animal carefully. Eleven in all, not counting Lolita and her filly. Some were of exceptional quality, and a few were a bit on the common side. A couple of the mares appeared quite heavy in foal.

He began to assign a horse to each young man, holding the tiger horse back for himself. The pretty sorrel mare was reserved for Standing Bird, absent now and in mourning for his parents. Heads Off instructed the youths in basic care and grooming. The enthusiasm of the Rabbits gave indication that the animals would be well cared for.

Next he explained the use of the horse's equipment. He showed them the bit, and demonstrated its use in the horse's mouth. Taking a clue from Coyote's interpretation, he explained the principles involved.

"This is the elk-dog medicine," he began, holding the bit aloft. "The circle around the lower jaw gives us the medicine that controls the elk-dog. Since I have only this one, we will use ropes for the other elk-dogs." He demonstrated the construction of the rope bridle such as they had already used on the foal, and previously at the time of acquisition of these horses.

Soon each animal had a makeshift bridle, and the boys were mounting and dismounting. Someone discovered that a rope tied loosely around the horse just behind the shoulders made it much easier to hold on. With this help, the young men were beginning to balance better and bounce less.

"Sit forward," Garcia repeatedly cautioned, and the bouncing decreased with more practice. A few spills brought uproarious laughter from the other youths. Practice with various gaits followed. At times Garcia despaired, but over the course of the next few days, he could see the beginnings of some riding skill emerging.

"Heads Off," asked a youthful member of the Hunter Society a few days later, "can you teach us to use the real-spear?"

An idea began to form in Garcia's mind. Why not, he

pondered, teach this group the use of the lance? They could easily learn to hunt buffalo, and with this sort of protection, the People need never fear the dreaded Head Splitters again. It would be hard, demanding work, teaching this raw group the skills of the academy, but what a fighting force they could be! He squatted in the now familiar position of rest and outlined his plan to eager young ears.

He sought out Stone Breaker and explained the need for the long spears. Each youngster was initially equipped with a wooden lance for practice, and was placed on his own responsibility for making or procuring a weapon for serious use.

In the coming days the group developed rapidly. Garcia constructed a number of hoops of willow, to be used as targets for the lances. Large at first, then progressively smaller as the budding warriors improved their skill. Soon all of the young men could neatly thread a circle no larger than a hand's span, dangling from a bush or tree, nearly every time.

An irregular course was prepared in the timber, and a rider would dash in zigzag pattern past the targets, attempting to collect the hoops on his lance shaft. This game appealed to the youngsters, but the biggest thrill for Garcia was a massed charge across the meadow. After one such demonstration, when every lance dangled a target hoop, he had to proudly concede that his little platoon was becoming pretty competent.

It was Coyote who whimsically dubbed the group the Elk-dog Society, and the young horsemen proudly adopted the name.

Several of the young men decided to try the use of the bow on horseback. Garcia was somewhat dubious of the idea. The bow was not his favorite weapon. Bowmen were traditionally foot soldiers. However, he was pleased to note that their charge could leave a grass-filled skin target well studded with arrows. This might work well on buffalo, he conceded.

All these new skills remained to be tested in actual practice, however. When the buffalo came, the Elk-dog Society could hardly be restrained. Garcia managed to control them into an orderly approach and a charge at gradually increasing speed. The results were spectacular. Nearly a dozen of the big animals fell before the lances and arrows of the horsemen.

When the People took the trail north, it was with a great deal of pride and confidence this year. The journey was without event, and the exuberant youngsters of the Elk-dog Society performed a wild demonstration of their new skills when the Southern band reached the site of the Sun Dance.

By the time of the Council two days later, people of other groups were referring to Hump Ribs' band as the Elk-dog band, and all the members were basking in new-found prestige. Hump Ribs' greeting to the Council was eagerly listened to by the other chiefs.

"I am Hump Ribs, chief of the Southern band," he began. "We have had a very big year."

He recounted the many events of the preceding year, the battle with the Head Splitters, and the chase and recovery of the captives. Hump Ribs was a good storyteller and knew how to give due credit to those mentioned in his story. The bravery of Mouse Roars received due mention, amid murmurs of regret. Mouse Roars had been one of the most respected of the sub-chiefs, and there were many to regret his passing.

It was grim news that the Head Splitters had obtained elk-dogs. Most of the bands had little contact with the Head Splitters because of their geographic distribution. There was some uneasy discussion as to whether the Head Splitters might be changing their range, encroaching on the land of the People. It was basically agreed that avoidance of contact would continue to be desirable. There was much approval of the successful foray, however.

When Hump Ribs led his group out of the big encampment at the end of the festivities, the Elk-dog band was larger by ten more lodges.

ᔑ 22 ᔐ

THREE of the newly acquired mares presented small elk-dogs in the next few weeks, increasing the size of the herd and promising to provide mounts for future Elk-dog soldiers. New uses were discovered for the animals. A couple of the youngsters discovered that a horse could drag a much heavier load on poles than any dog. Moving became appreciably easier for those families fortunate enough to have the use of the horses.

The band traveled southwest after leaving the Sun Dance, for the purpose of obtaining new lodge poles. This route took them into less familiar country, and this might account for their totally unexpected encounter with a moving band of Head Splitters. As in the previous year, with women and children present, both groups desired to avoid conflict.

The two detachments of chiefs and warriors squared off for an apparently friendly greeting. Garcia looked over the other band, noting their size, the probable number of warriors. They had a couple of horses, he noted, but were using them only for pack animals. He believed this band to be a different group than the one involved in the battle.

Coyote was nudging him with an elbow, and he returned his attention to the conversation of the chiefs. Hump Ribs was talking, with spoken words and sign language.

"Yes," he continued, "it was a good fight." The irritation of the Head Splitters was obvious, and left no doubt as to which fight was under discussion. Men gripped weapons tightly.

"You have yet to learn," answered the Head Splitter chief. "It was the son of our real-chief that your Hair Face killed. Gray Wolf has sworn that he will decorate his shield with that fur." He gestured toward Garcia.

It was a tense moment. A false or provocative move on the part of either group could have precipitated a blood bath. Into the midst of the deadly quiet tension intruded Coyote's high-pitched giggle.

"I have heard it said," he observed to no one in particular, "that to use a cat's skin you must first skin the cat."

Several men of the People chuckled, relieving the

tension somewhat. Coyote had not accompanied his observation with sign language, and much of the implication was lost on the Head Splitters. The two groups cautiously backed off and circled away.

Garcia now spent some time in serious thought. He had been thinking primarily in terms of hunting skills for his young horsemen. Now he must concede that eventually they would be committed to combat. He began to notice the heavy rawhide shields carried by some of the men. They were made of the thick skin from the backs of large bulls. The dried rawhide, laced to a hoop of dogwood or hickory as it cured, was as hard as iron. It could easily turn the point of an arrow or spear. Perhaps a slightly smaller version could be useful on horseback.

The possibilities were apparent to others when he mentioned it, and several young men soon sported shields as they practiced their skill with the lance. It became a symbol of prestige to hang the shield in front of one's lodge.

All in all, Garcia was rather proud of the season's accomplishments. His main frustration concerned his upcoming marriage. This waiting was not at all what he had had in mind. Tall One continued to send seductive glances in his direction, and to touch him lightly whenever opportunity offered. In turn, he could hardly keep his hands from her willowy body. She tolerated a certain amount of contact, but always gently restrained him when his advances became too amorous. The young man was unsure just what rights and privileges were customary with his present status. He didn't want to break any of the tribal taboos, but he longed to get the girl alone for a while.

Meanwhile, the women sewed skins together and prepared numerous articles to be ready for the new lodge. The band had moved southwest after the Sun Dance, to spend some time in the place of lodge poles. Most lodges were in need of a few replacement poles, and it was generally understood that the new lodge of Heads Off and the Tall One must be constructed of the finest new materials.

The cottonwoods grew thickly along the flat level bottoms. Some were no thicker than his arm, yet as tall as several men before the first branches broke the smooth surface. The People harvested and peeled many lodge poles during the next few suns.

Finally Hump Ribs called for the move, and the band moved southward, to winter in a generally new area. An area, it became apparent, where the union of Heads Off and his bride would take place. The bright new lodge was erected near that of Coyote, but Heads Off was warned not to enter.

"You must wait until everything is finished," Big Footed Woman chided. He could see that the lodge was presumptuous, perhaps taller than any except that of Hump Ribs himself.

Finally a Warriors' Dance was announced. The occasion would be doubly significant, it was understood, since following the ceremonies Heads Off would take his bride.

It appeared that Heads Off was expected to participate in the dance. Reluctantly and somewhat embarrassed, he attempted the rhythmic shuffling step of the warriors. He remembered some of the songs from the previous year, but found that as the ceremony wore on, some were new songs. There was one about the bravery of Mouse Roars, and that of old Black Dog.

Suddenly, Garcia realized that one song was about his own exploits. His killing of buffalo was mentioned, his elk-dog medicine, and the encounter with the Head Splitters. His part in the pursuit and raid was a part of the story, as was the acquisition of the elk-dogs.

Near the end of this portion of the dance, Tall One stepped gracefully forward to confront him. She placed articles of beautifully decorated clothing at his feet. Remembering the ritual, Garcia stopped and planted his lance. People came forward to accept the gifts, while the embarrassed young man blushed at all the attention.

It seemed the festivities would never end, but finally after the last mock battle and the last charge across the arena, the Warriors' Dance was over. Coyote stepped forward, savoring the moment of glory, and placed the hand of Tall One in that of her husband. He spread a soft-tanned robe around the shoulders of the couple, enveloping both.

Garcia thought the girl had never looked lovelier than this evening. Her white buckskin dress was intricately decorated with quillwork, and her hair carefully braided and bound with strips of fur. She took his hand and led him to the bright new lodge.

Inside, a fire was burning. By its light, the bridegroom looked around at his new home. Starting to one side of the doorway, painted figures marched around the lining. Numerous small buffalo were dominated by a bearded figure on an elk-dog, who brandished a long spear over them. Further around was a battle scene, in which the same bearded figure thrust a lance through a warrior on a spotted horse. On the next skin, accompanied by two smaller horsemen, he led several captured horses by ropes.

It was like watching his life for the past two years. Beyond that, the skin lodge lining was blank, reserved for future deeds.

"Heads Off!" a soft voice called him back to reality. He turned. A bed of soft robes had been prepared, directly across from the doorway.

"Heads Off, my husband," Tall One repeated seductively, "come to me."

❧ 23 ❧

G ARCIA opened his eyes and looked cautiously at the head pillowed comfortably on his bare shoulder. Her long lashes lay on the dark skin of her cheeks, and she smiled, gently stirring in her sleep. Her silky hair fell across his neck and shoulder. She snuggled closer under the robe, moving a warm knee across his thighs. He held very still, not wanting to awaken her. Yet he could not avoid becoming aroused.

They had moved into their own lodge a week ago. The ensuing days had been the most perfect that young Garcia could have imagined. Tall One's eager responsiveness was beyond his most imaginative daydreams. The sensuous gaze of her large dark eyes in the firelight was such a flattering boost to his ego that he felt like the greatest man in the world.

He smiled to himself as he watched a shaft of sunlight creep through the smoke hole at the top of the lodge. He could hardly believe that he had, a few short weeks ago, considered himself a prisoner of circumstances. A life like this, a prison? He sighed a contented sigh, and wondered what the People were thinking. He and Tall One had barely been outside the lode. He was sure that the Elk-dog Society would be making ribald jokes about the absence of Heads Off from the daily practice sessions. Well, let them have their jokes. They were probably envious.

He thought with amusement of some of the prominent chiefs. Hump Ribs, for instance, with six wives. How could such a thing be? Hump Ribs couldn't possibly handle that many wives, could he? Garcia was certain that none of these was a wife anything like Tall One. He could barely keep up with her desires himself, and he had always regarded himself as fairly well endowed in that respect.

He became aware that the large dark eyes were open and gazing into his face. That look of adoration again, lifting him to greatness.

"Are you happy, my husband?" she whispered.

He nodded, smiled, and gave her a quick little squeeze.

"Are you?"

"Of course! No woman could have a braver, stronger

man. And as a husband?" She raised her brows in mock alarm, and looked over at the paintings on the lodge lining. "I have been thinking. Maybe we should have another picture about your deeds in bed."

Garcia was momentarily alarmed. Did they really paint picture stories about that? Then he realized she was laughing at him. He slapped her playfully on the buttocks and pulled her to him.

Not all their shared pleasures were to be in bed, however. In the warm afternoons of the Falling Leaves the two took long walks together. Tall One seemed a sensuous woman, skilled in the ways of womankind. Yet at the same time, she was like a happy child, thrilled at every sight and sound of beauty.

She was unpredictable, too. They were walking one day and she suddenly spoke.

"I can beat you to the top of the hill!"

She lifted her buckskin skirt and sprinted away, long legs flashing. The dumbfounded young man recovered from his surprise and dashed after her. He was amazed at how fast the girl could run. Even though he was in excellent condition, he was panting hard by the time they slowed and tumbled together into the soft grass at the hilltop.

The lovers shared the thrill of watching wild geese as the long lines in perfect geometric formation beat their way southward. They enjoyed the beauty of the first autumn leaves as they turned crimson and gold. They watched a coyote pup become completely confused over the tricks of a pair of experienced rabbits. The long-ears had run in a big circle, trading off each circuit while the other rested. The young coyote finally gave up, tired and hungry, and ambled off to look for easier prey. Garcia and Tall One laughed like children at the pup's puzzled glance back over his shoulder.

The girl showed him many things, as the sunlight grew shorter in the Moon of Falling Leaves. She loved to watch small fish in the quiet pools of the river, and birds in the grassy meadows. They once spent some time simply lying in the sun and watching a hawk with a red tail draw perfect circles in the hazy afternoon sky.

Garcia began to realize that he had been overlooking a great deal that the People considered important. The prairie itself, he had regarded as merely something to be crossed to arrive at one's destination. Now, through the shared experiences with his wife, he began to feel something of the attitude of the People. Far from being a lifeless plain, the prairie became for him, as for his wife's people, a living thing. Throbbing, alive, pulsating with the reality of all creation, the timeless prairie landscape was becoming a part of his life. How could he have missed the overwhelming importance of the Sun Dance, he thought. There was a ceremony expressing the entire thing, an idea too great for words.

The two young people stood watching Sun Boy carry his torch over the rim of the world. Amid a dazzling display of scarlet and gold and orange, streaks of purple and smoky blue began to herald the approach of twilight. Garcia felt that he had never experienced such a oneness with his Creator. Somehow, he doubted if the padre would have understood, and he was a little embarrassed. They turned, arms around each other's waists, to stroll back to the village.

With a heightened awareness of surroundings, Garcia began to notice other customs of the People, also. He chanced to see White Buffalo, after an especially successful hunt, carrying out a simple ritual. The old man had taken a well-cleaned buffalo skull. On the broad forehead he had painted a circular design of red and yellow, a design used often by the People. The skull was placed on an outcropping of stone near the hilltop. White Buffalo stepped back and solemnly addressed the skull as if he were talking to a friend.

"We are sorry to kill you, my brother," he began, "but we thank you for our food and shelter, and for the things we wear. May your people go on forever, as long as the grass grows and the wind blows."

Turning, the medicine man shuffled back to his lodge, leaving the decorated skull to the elements. It was, Garcia realized, another simple acknowledgment of the interdependence of the People with all of creation.

Eventually, the young lovers began to spend less time together. Garcia returned to his Elk-dog trainees, and Tall One to her wifely occupations of sewing, cooking, and making a comfortable lodge for her man. Both continued to enjoy the time they shared, however. Every time Garcia turned his steps toward his lodge, it was with eager anticipation, and he resented the time they spent apart.

Occasionally, he would daydream. What a thrill it would be, he would imagine in his fantasy, to introduce his wife to his family and friends. He could visualize her dusky beauty, emphasized by a well-fitted white satin dress of the latest fashion. She would enter the big dining room on his arm and every head would turn. Everyone would gasp at the striking looks of the beautiful foreign wife of young Juan Garcia.

Yet he knew that this could not be. The girl could never adapt to the customs of civilization, and he could not ask her to. She would be out of her element, like a fish out of water. She was a wild and free spirit, in close communion with the prairie that was her home. And he felt that he had been privileged to be included in this communion. By his union with this woman, he now realized, he had given up all possibility of returning to his previous life.

And that, he considered, snuggling against her warm body, was a fair exchange.

ᥒ 24 ᥓ

THAT WINTER was as hard and bitter as the previous one had been mild and open. Sun Boy and Cold Maker waged a daily battle, watched eagerly by the People.

By tradition, Coyote related, Sun Boy's torch becomes old and nearly goes out every winter. This winter it seemed it must really go out permanently. Even on days when the sunlight was in evidence, it failed to warm. The pale, watery yellow rays barely began to warm the surface of the frozen drifts before sinking again below the earth's rim.

Sun Boy had been pushed far to the south, Coyote

pointed out, and was barely able to run half way up across the sky. His low arching path was hardly able to combat the might of the Cold Maker. Never before, said the old ones, had Cold Maker had such strong medicine. Never had the snow come so often and so deep. There was a time in the Moon of Long Nights when Cold Maker was victorious in the daily combat for more days than one has fingers and toes. Sun Boy was not seen in all of this time. And close behind came the Snow Moon and the Hunger Moon.

It was during this time that one old woman wandered off into the storm and was lost. She had apparently gone into the timber along the river, and simply failed to return. Her body was not found until the drifts began to melt in the Wakening Moon. She was curled in a comfortable sleeping position beneath a bush only a hundred paces behind her own family's lodge, her small bundle of sticks beside her small body.

"Cold Maker is a liar," observed Coyote. "He tells his victims that all is well, and they will be warm and comfortable if they only lie down to rest a little."

There were many attempts at explanations for the hard winter. It might be, said some of the chronic complainers, that they were camped in the wrong place. Hump Ribs' band had rarely wintered this far to the west, and some said Cold Maker was displeased at the invasion into his mountain domain. Others were afraid Sun Boy was angry, and ready to punish or even abandon the People. Perhaps the Sun Dance had been ineffective, for reasons not understood.

White Buffalo tried hard to help the situation with

songs and dances of entreaty. His drum could be heard at odd hours, early and late. He withdrew himself to his lodge to use all his medicine in the attempt to avert disaster. Sometimes it did seem that on the days following the medicine man's late night efforts, Sun Boy's torch was somewhat brighter. But again, Garcia wondered, was it only because White Buffalo was extremely adept at reading the sign of coming weather changes? He said nothing, but suspected that Coyote also had noted this possibility. No matter, he decided, White Buffalo was a respected man, doing his job well.

It must be noted that there were a few of the chronic skeptics and grumblers who whispered another possible cause of the disaster. Such weather had never been known to the People, they murmured in private conversations, until the coming of the elk-dogs and the unorthodox methods of hunting.

Standing Bird was furious as he overheard one of the conversations.

"And you have never," he sputtered in rage to the grumblers, "spent a winter with such full bellies and sleeping in so many warm robes until the coming of Heads Off and the elk-dogs!"

This could not be denied. The People, though depressed and uncomfortable, were in no acute danger from Cold Maker's onslaught. They heaped snow around the lodges, stuffed dry grass into the space behind the lodge linings for warmth, and settled into a routine around the lodge fires. Fresh meat was furnished by the dogs, for occasional relief from dried meat and pemmican. For once, Hunger Moon was not marked by hunger.

Pathways through the snow led from lodge to lodge, packed down by the traffic. Long evenings of activity took place as friends gathered in each other's lodges. The social smokes were sometimes combined with gambling sessions.

The People were dedicated gamblers, Garcia decided. Small children, he had noticed before, frequently played the stick game when the weather prevented outside play. Their version was simply a "which hand" guess, such as he had played as a child. Coyote's younger children had been delighted during his first winter with them to find that Garcia knew the game, and would play it with them occasionally.

He had also noticed that some of the People would bet on anything. There were some compulsive gamblers who would see two birds in a tree and bet on which would fly first. Not too much different than some of the wastrels he had known, Garcia thought. One young man in the group was continually bordering on poverty with his obsessive gambling. This bothered him not a bit. Some day he would win big, he assured Garcia.

Garcia was far from being a moralist himself. Still, he felt that if the young gambler would devote as much time to his weapons and hunting practice as to his gambling, he wouldn't need the big win. Garcia felt a bit sorry for the young wife, who tried to struggle along with a near-poverty existence.

The games of chance did provide a useful diversion during the depressing Long Nights Moon. Friends could spend an evening with the plum stones, and forget that Cold Maker howled outside.

One side of each plum seed was painted red, and an odd-numbered handful would be shaken and tossed on a robe, with wagers on the proportion of red to yellow seeds showing.

Best of all that winter, however, were the long nights when there were no smokes, no games of the plum stones, and no visitors. Garcia would go outside to relieve himself before retiring for the night, and stand for a moment to look across the camp. The dull red-amber glow shone through the skin lodge covers, and reflected on the snow. The effect was pleasing, he thought, but he lost no time retreating from the chilling wind and into the warm comfortable lodge.

He and Tall One spent long hours talking and laughing about nothing, and seemed never to run out of the small nothings to discuss. And of course, they spent long nights snuggled closely together against the winter's chill.

Eventually, Sun Boy did triumph, of course. He always does, in the end, Coyote stated, though he confessed that even he had had his doubts this year. But the drifted snow did melt, and in the Wakening Moon the cry of geese heading north was heard again in the night sky. The People came out of the lodges and began to resume more normal activity.

To his amazement, Garcia discovered a change in the personality of his wife. Most of the People had changed, to be sure. They changed from bitter, quarrelsome, and dejected to happy, laughing individuals as warm south winds drove Cold Maker back to the mountains.

With Tall One it was the opposite. She became grumpy and tearful, her cooking and her management of the lodge became slipshod and careless. She cried easily, and when her husband attempted to comfort her, became downright angry. More time was spent in her bed, but she definitely did not want his company. Where he formerly had experienced warm soft curves and welcoming embraces, now he encountered only knees and elbows.

Occasionally she repented, and made love to him almost fiercely. At his next attempt, however, he would meet total rejection. At one especially frustrating episode, his attempts to stroke and fondle met with angry accusations and tears. Garcia retreated, hurt, angry, and confused. Could this be the same sensuous creature who had shared his bed during the Moon of Long Nights? He sought out his father-in-law to ask advice.

"Coyote, I would like to speak with you," began the dejected young man. "It is about Tall One."

Coyote methodically finished the piece of meat he was gnawing, tossed the bone to the dogs, and wiped the grease from his hands on his leggings.

"Come, let us walk," he suggested.

Garcia poured forth all his frustration and disappointment as they strolled outside the camp. Coyote nodded soberly.

"Have I made her unhappy? Is there some custom of the People that I do not understand?"

Coyote shook his head.

"I think not, Heads Off. It is always like this when a woman is with child."

"With *child?*" The possibility had not even occurred to him. He had not extended his thinking far enough to include children in his lodge. He was still thinking in terms of a perpetual honeymoon.

"Of course," Coyote was saying. "How could it be otherwise? The two of you have hardly left your lodge since the Moon of Falling Leaves."

❧ 25 ❧

WITH AN UNDERSTANDING of the nature of the problem came almost instant answers. Garcia became so solicitous of his wife's well-being that she was almost embarrassed. This did indeed help her attitude, but she was already nearly past the uncomfortable weeks of early pregnancy. Tall One did still require extra sleep, but her depressed moods improved, and she became more like her previous self. A restoration of their happy friendship was a great relief to Garcia. As his attentiveness increased, so did their closeness.

Early in the Greening Moon, the People fired the dry prairie grass. For several nights, the sky was lighted by the orange reflections of flame on billowing clouds of white smoke. The blackened prairie smoldered in spots, and the smell of the fires was in everyone's nostrils for days. Soon, after a warm spring rain, sprouts of green began to appear among the sooty stubble. In a week the rolling hills were covered with a lush emerald-green. This, promised Coyote, would attract great herds of buffalo.

Garcia had taken a walk alone to the top of the hill to examine the results of the burn and to look for the herds. Among the blackened shards of last year's grass he found a myriad of tiny white flowers. He remembered that the women of his culture admired a gift of flowers, and impulsively gathered a handful of the pointed, ivory-colored blooms.

"They are beautiful, Heads Off," Tall One murmured appreciatively as she buried her nose in the tiny cluster. "We call these the dog-tooth. They always follow the fire."

He was learning to touch her sensitive nature and her appreciation of beauty. Their relationship became better than ever. How very much better, he noted with relief, then at the height of their misunderstanding.

The herds did come, and hunting was good. Garcia had forgotten how good the taste of fresh buffalo meat could be. The young men of the Elk-dog Society gloried in the ability to provide for their lodges, and large quantities of meat were obtained.

One curious thing occurred. Garcia noticed that the women of the butchering parties would slice an occasional morsel of liver and pop it into their mouths as they worked. He did not recall seeing this before. The liver was not easily stored, so was usually eaten immediately, but usually cooked. The consumption of raw bites while still warm was puzzling. He asked Tall One about it.

"I do not know, Heads Off," she answered around a mouthful of the delicacy. Her hands and forearms were smeared with blood as she smiled up at him from her work. "It seems a good thing after a hard winter. It has always been so. Here! Try some!"

She sliced off a morsel and handed it to him. Gingerly, he tried it. Not bad, to his surprise. In fact, aside from the unpleasant texture, there was something very satisfying about it. A great deal like the satisfaction of a craving for fresh vegetables after a tedious diet of meats through the winter. He watched Tall One ravenously devouring another bit. There must be some sustenance there that her body needs for the child, he mused, watching other women follow the same course of action.

The People had secured almost as much food before the time to move as would be obtained in a normal year prior to the elk-dogs. They were looking forward to the annual Sun Dance festival. It would be such a satisfaction to arrive in all the prosperity that was now the status of the Elk-dog band.

The horses had continued to multiply, and a sizable number of foals and yearlings would make the journey to the Big Council. Several animals had changed hands, through gift, barter, and in one case, loss through a wager. No matter, thought Hump Ribs proudly. His would be the wealthiest band at the Council. All his life he had been a member, later a chief, of the smallest band of the People. Now, in a space of a few summers, they had become one of the largest. Certainly the wealthiest. He could feel the weight of shifting prestige as more lodges had joined him each year.

And this was the best year yet. The chief was already daydreaming of their arrival in splendor. Perhaps this was a factor in his decision for an early move.

The usual protest arose from the women. They couldn't possibly be ready in three days. The meat from the recent kill was not yet prepared. Even while they protested, they started preparations for the move.

Big Footed Woman was among the most vocal of the protesters. It was foolish, she scolded, to think that all the fat from the recent kills could possibly be cooked down properly in so short a time. Mere men, even chiefs, could not understand such a problem. Just because times were now improved was no cause to become wasteful. Good food had never been wasted by the People, even in times of plenty. She, for one, would never leave meat on the prairie to rot. She had no intention, she continued, of leaving this camp site until her work was done. The men wisely refrained from argument.

Nevertheless, on the appointed morning, the lodge of Coyote came down with all the rest. Long Elk and the younger children helped with the packing, using some of the horses to transport the lodge covers of both their lodge and that of Heads Off and Tall One.

By noon the last of the lodges was packed and on the move. Coyote and his son-in-law deliberately avoided that portion of the band where their family traveled. It seemed advisable to avoid any unnecessary exposure to the sharp tongue of Big Footed Woman. Let her vent her wrath, and by evening perhaps her temper would be cooled enough to make life livable again.

It was a pleasant half day's travel, and as the band prepared to camp for the night, the men ventured to seek out the family. Long Elk and the children were preparing a camp site, and had a fire going.

"Where is your mother?" asked Coyote. Apprehensive looks greeted him.

"She stayed behind to finish cooking her fat," stated Long Elk apologetically. "She said they would catch up. Tall One is with her."

Garcia wasn't sure whether to be angry, to laugh, or to be fearful for their safety. He had had no idea that Big Footed Woman would go so far to make her point. Apparently Coyote hadn't either. And Tall One, staying with her. Garcia wasn't sure whether she was trying to prove the same thing, being loyal to her mother, or staying because of anxiety, not wanting to leave her mother alone.

In any case, it had become a dangerous situation. Night was falling, and there was no sign of the women. After brief discussion, it was decided that Garcia and Long Elk would ride back to meet them, and help carry their ridiculous cooking fat.

∂ 26 ∕

SHADOWS were becoming long over the abandoned camp site, but one fire still burned.

"Mother, we *must* leave! Please forget the rest of the fat," Tall One entreated. She had stayed behind to help finish the cooking and to help with the carrying. She had had no idea that her mother would stay this long over her silly grudge.

Actually, Big Footed Woman hadn't intended it this way. She would, she thought, let them leave without her. She was certain that the men would come back as soon as their absence was discovered. She would then grudgingly consent to leave, having proved her argument.

But the men had not come. Her anger was rekindled, and her stubborn streak began to manifest itself even more strongly. She would stay here until they did come, she decided.

But that was while the sun still shone. Now the darkness was falling, and the whole thing began to seem a little foolish. Maybe they should pack up and travel, she thought. They could follow the trail of the entire band, even in complete darkness. She was about to capitulate, and in fact had drawn in her breath to speak, when Tall One held up a hand to listen.

Unmistakably, there was a sound of hoofbeats. Three or four elk-dogs at a walk, were approaching. Both women brightened considerably, and Big Footed Woman began to plan her scathing remarks for the men. She turned her back and began paying utmost attention to skimming melted grease and spooning it out to cool.

"Here they come," she murmured, savoring her moment. The horses came closer, up to the very edge of the firelight, and stopped. She heard a chuckle, but not until a gasp of surprise and fear came from Tall

One did she turn.

There were four men, each sitting on his horse in a relaxed, amused posture. They made no immediate move, merely sat, smiling and chuckling. It took a long moment for the significance of the situation to make itself felt to Big Footed Woman. Somehow her mind was slow to grasp so unexpected a scene. She had been certain that when she turned she would see her husband and Heads Off.

But these men were complete strangers. And by their ornaments and weapons, Big Footed Woman could see that her bull-headed escapade had backfired. These men were not even of the People.

They were Head Splitters.

"Hello, Mother," signed the oldest of the Head Splitters, apparently the leader. "Is our supper ready?"

Foolishly though she had acted that day, Big Footed Woman was wise enough not to do anything foolish in that moment. If either of the women rocked the delicately balanced situation, the results might be an instant tragedy. As it was, the Head Splitters seemed to be enjoying the game. Their only chance, both women realized, was to play along and stall for time.

"Get down and sit," signed Big Footed Woman. "You are early. My husband will be back soon."

Laughter from the Head Splitters. They could see that the camp was abandoned. They slid from the horses and wandered around the fire, poking at the strips of fat.

"Get away from my cooking," the woman spoke irritably, reinforcing her demand with sign language and a gentle shove. "I will say when it is ready!" More laughter.

It's working she thought. We will be safe as long as I can keep them laughing. Maybe the men will come.

Of course, both women knew that their cause was hopeless. They could feed the strangers, and for some time possibly dissuade them. Eventually the Head Splitters would tire of the game, and would kill them, probably after raping them. Already the small one with teeth like those of a squirrel was roving his glance over the long body of Tall One. The best that might happen would be that they would take her with them instead of killing her outright. Too bad, thought Big Footed Woman. I did want her to bear the child of Heads Off.

Even while her mind was busy with such morose thoughts, her hands were busy with the cooking fire. She chattered on in a combination of talk and sign.

"Stay back, you'll kick dirt in my cooking!" she ordered.

The Head Splitters were enjoying this scene immensely. One of them made an exaggerated move to escape her scolding, and the others rocked with laughter. Big Footed Woman began to cook some small strips of meat, and hand the morsels to the men. She wondered how much she could prolong this process. She cooked small portions, and only a few at a time, assisted by Tall One, who had thus far been silent.

Full darkness fell, and the process of cooking and feeding the strangers continued. Tall One kindled a torch and propped it nearby for light. Once the older man impatiently demanded that they cook bigger portions.

"Mother," finally spoke Tall One, "don't you think that little one looks like a squirrel?" Tall One glanced at the little man. Complete absence of any understanding shone on all four faces as they chewed pieces of meat or joked among themselves.

Her mother nodded. "And the big one is the ugliest I ever saw." The big one in question smiled and nodded.

"I thought so," concluded Tall One. "None of them understands a word of the talk of the People. Now I will tell you my idea. I do not intend to go to bed with Squirrel Tooth over there." She smiled at the man again, and he responded with a toothy grin.

Rapidly, Tall One sketched her plan, and her mother nodded.

"It is good. Even if it does not work, we may escape in the darkness."

Finally it seemed that the nearly insatiable appetites were becoming satisfied. Squirrel Tooth was looking hungrily at Tall One. It was time to make a move. Tall One strolled over to replace the sputtering torch with a fresh one. Instead of propping it for light, she suddenly lifted it high and dashed off into the darkness, the flame bobbing and dancing over her head.

The Head Splitters leaped to their feet and ran after her, shouting to each other as they ran. Big Footed Woman quickly picked up a heavy stone war club and slipped into the darkness.

Tall One ran down the familiar path, counting on the unfamiliarity of her pursuers with the terrain. She looked back, slowing her pace slightly. It was important that the pursuit be as close as possible. The line of flight led straight across a flat, level area with no obstructions, and her long legs kept her barely ahead of the running warriors. She wondered if they thought her stupid to be carrying the torch.

A hundred paces behind the abandoned lodge site, the level meadow dropped off sharply to the river. The edge was a shelf of stone, jutting out of the earth and ending abruptly. Below lay a tangled pile of jagged pieces broken from the shelf through the centuries and dropped into the stream's bed.

Straight for the edge ran Tall One. As she neared the drop, she sprinted faster, pulling slightly away from the runners behind. She waved the torch high, then suddenly flung it ahead of her and dodged quickly to the left, slipping quietly into a clump of bushes. The plan worked perfectly. The men, in full stride, continued to pursue the bobbing, flashing torch as it bounced over the rocks. The two in the lead did not even break stride as they plunged over the edge. It seemed a long time before the dull sound of their bodies striking rock was heard. The third man, Squirrel Tooth, realized something was wrong just as he reached the ledge. He attempted to save himself, but overbalanced and fell, a short exclamation of surprise choked off by the dull thud.

The fourth man was warned, and managed to stop at the edge. He called into the dark, but there was only a low moan for answer. The torch lay far below, flickering in a crevice near the water. He turned to look for the girl, shouting angrily. Tall One hugged the earth and tried not to breathe too heavily.

"Tall One!" a voice called from the darkness. "Bring the big ugly one back to the fire and let him catch you, almost!"

The big man turned toward the voice, but the girl jumped up with a frightened squeal and ran back toward the fire, the warrior in hot pursuit. She dodged around, barely staying out of his reach, until she saw, from the corner of her vision, where her mother was located. Twisting, turning, the agile young woman maneuvered her pursuer into proper position, and finally stumbled, sprawling with a little scream.

The man loomed over her in a rage, and his hands reached for the girl. She was very glad that he had no weapon. At the last moment there was a dull thunk, and the Head Splitter slumped forward, falling almost on top of her. Big Footed Woman brushed the hair back from her face as she hefted the borrowed war club in case another blow was needed. It was not.

The exhausted women made their way back to the fire. As they built the blaze up, they suddenly heard hoofbeats again, and both slipped warily into the darkness.

Garcia and Long Elk rode into the circle of the firelight and paused, calling their names. Big Footed Woman stepped quickly from hiding.

"Heads Off, Long Elk! Over here," she called. They returned to the fire.

"Mother!" shouted Long Elk. "We were very worried!"

"Oh, we are all right," she managed to say calmly. "We traded meat to some travelers for four elk-dogs." She pointed to the animals, tied in the shadows.

Garcia was irritated. He had been nearly frantic with worry, and did not appreciate the light treatment of a near tragedy.

"Come on," he snapped gruffly. "Let us join the rest."

"Of course, Heads Off," answered his wife meekly, "as soon as we finish skimming out the fat."

ॐ 27 ॐ

T HE INCIDENT had been revealing in a number of ways. Most important was the fact that the Head Splitters not only possessed horses, but were using them regularly. Garcia had hoped that the attack of the previous year had been a freak occurrence, an exception to the usual. He had been reinforced in that thinking by the fact that the attackers had seemed inexperienced, unfamiliar with their mounts.

He questioned Tall One carefully about the men involved in last night's escapade. They had been experienced warriors, without a doubt. He had examined the captured horses closely. The Head Splitters had used a similar arrangement for control of the animal to that he and Coyote had devised. A thong through the mouth, in lieu of a bit. The other equipment was even more revealing. One animal had a rawhide saddle pad, stuffed with dried grass. Moreover, the pad showed a great deal of discoloration from long use, sweat, and dust. It had been used for some time. This would indicate that the elk-dogs had been in the possession of this band of Head Splitters for a while. This was no chance acquisition.

Supporting this insight was the fact that two of the other horses were wearing rawhide boots. A very good idea, he thought, to protect against the sharp flint and limestone of the rimrock. He called this to the attention of the Elk-dog Society. A couple of the young men whose horses had had trouble with tender feet were quick to experiment with the idea.

The major fact sank home with a bit of a threat, however. With the Head Splitters using horses as a regular occurrence, the People were in constant danger of attack. War parties of the enemy could move rapidly and far. At no time would there be complete freedom from fear of attack.

Garcia mentioned this to Coyote and the two of them sought out the chief to discuss this potential problem. Hump Ribs listened intently, and then proposed to call a council.

The warriors gathered in front of Hump Ribs' lodge as darkness fell, and the council fire was lighted. Outside the circle of warriors were the younger men and boys, and a number of interested women. The ceremonial pipe was lighted and passed, and finally Hump Ribs spoke to open the discussion.

"My brothers," he began, "a thing has come to be which may be a danger to the People. I have asked Heads Off to tell you of it."

Garcia cleared his throat, every eye upon him.

"My brothers," he scarcely realized how easily the phrase came now, "two of our women have had an encounter with the Head Splitters." A chuckle ran round the circle. The story of the incident and its outcome was well known.

"We have captured four more elk-dogs. But, our danger is this. The Head Splitters may be using elk-dogs more and more."

The murmur in the circle was now one of doubt and apprehension as he continued.

"These men used the elk-dogs well. They are no more, but there are more Head Splitters where they came from. They can now move far and fast. The People could be attacked at any time."

Confused, argumentative discussion followed, tempers flared. Once again, Garcia was impressed that the basic tone of the discussion was that of run-and-hide, rather than of defense in strength. He despaired trying to explain the difference in approach that he felt necessary. His command of the language was still somewhat limited.

There was a strong faction who argued in favor of joining one of the other bands of the People for mutual defense. This would be possible, they insisted, because of the more affluent position of the band. More buffalo were now available to the People with less effort because of the elk-dogs. Two Pines, originally of the Red Rocks band, favored this approach. In spite of his great ability as a hunter and a warrior, there were some who resented the man as an outsider.

Someone hotly accused him of self-serving motives

if the group joined the Red Rock band. Two Pines became silent and angry, obviously hurt by the accusation. The council was deteriorating rapidly into a conflict of personalities.

Hump Ribs held up a hand for silence. Sometimes the responsibility of his position could weigh heavily. He sighed inwardly. Perhaps his friend Coyote could soothe some injured feelings with his sense of humor. The chief turned to the little man. Coyote had thus far been silent, listening intently to the discussion. His eyes darted from one speaker to the other.

"Coyote, you have not yet spoken."

"Yes, my chief. I am puzzled. Why do we sit, and say 'Aiee, the head Splitters have elk-dogs,' when we also have elk-dogs? Let the Head Splitters sit and say, 'Aiee, the *People* have elk-dogs'!" He paused a moment for the idea to take full effect, and Hump Ribs was once again impressed with the little man's uncanny sense of timing.

"I am told," Coyote continued, "by our brother, Heads off, the elk-dogs are often used among his people for fighting. They can be strength for us as easily as for the Head Splitters. Already our young men are skilled in their use for hunting. They can as easily use their elk-dogs for fighting."

Something very like a cheer came from the ranks of younger warriors in the rear. The older men of the council attempted to look with stern disapproval on such levity, but with difficulty. The air of pride and success was contagious.

"Also, we have fought the Head Splitters and beaten

them. We have stolen their elk-dogs. Even our women"—Coyote giggled, unable to resist the reference to the triumph of his wife and daughter—"have shown that the Head Splitters are no match for the People!"

The entire council was now relaxed, laughing, happy, and proud. Garcia had come to admire his father-in-law's ability to handle people, but this was beyond his understanding. How, in just a few moments, could this have happened? From a bickering, angry crowd composed of several factions, Coyote had somehow formed a cohesive group, whose members stood tall with pride.

Garcia felt a presence at his elbow, and turned to see White Buffalo. The old man's eyes twinkled with amusement.

"Sometimes," observed the medicine man, "a real leader is one who can lead without appearing to." He looked around the circle, and chuckled quietly at the noisy enthusiasm. "They think this was their idea!"

The exuberance continued, until Hump Ribs finally raised his hand again.

"It is well, my brothers. But we must do more than talk. Now, let us plan."

Discussion progressed at a more deliberate and productive pace. It would be important, it was agreed, to be forewarned of any enemy attack. With this in mind, a system of sentries was established. A surprise attack like the one of the previous year should be preventable with proper attention to the watch.

One further subject came under discussion. The subject of the Head Splitters and their elk-dogs must be brought before the Big Council at the Sun Dance.

◈ 28 ◈

THE SUN DANCE that year was held at Walnut Creek, one of the traditional gathering spots for the tribe. It was apparent from the time of arrival of Hump Ribs' band that change was in the air. Prior to this time, the elk-dogs were a curiosity, something to marvel at and make jokes about. A useful curiosity, perhaps. Some among the People had seen their usefulness very early. Others had failed to grasp the significance.

Now, there could no longer be any doubt. The Southern band of Hump Ribs, now called the Elk-dog band, arrived for the Sun Dance in splendor. Others of the People marveled at the ease with which the elk-dog people were able to transport heavy lodge covers and bulky baggage. And what quantities of possessions! They had obviously wintered well. The children were fat and active, and the women were happy. All of Hump Ribs' band were well dressed and well armed. The remarkable medicine of the elk-dogs was obviously responsible.

If there had been any doubt of this, it was dispelled by the spectacular sight of the Elk-dog Society. They wheeled and paraded in a show of splendor that sent a thrill of excitement down the backs of the People. There was a proud demeanor in the attitude of the elk-dog group that did not go unnoticed by the other chiefs.

At the Big Council, there was excitement in the air. The big news was that the Red Rocks band had been attacked in their winter camp. Their usual range was close to that territory claimed by the Head Splitters, but traditionally, only sporadic raids had occurred. This had been a full-scale attack, just as the weather had opened up in the Wakening Moon.

The men had been on an early spring hunt, replenishing supplies after a hard winter. The village was largely unprotected when the horsemen swooped down, killing and burning. The few older warriors present had made a brave stand, but were swept away by the force of the enemy. Many children were stolen, and there was scarcely a lodge that was not in mourning. The pitiful remnants of the band were thin, ragged, and in poor condition. Most of their possessions had been looted or burned.

White Bear, chief of the once-proud Red Rocks band, presented in almost hopeless narrative. Many of their people had been killed or had joined other bands, he noted, glancing ruefully at Hump Ribs. The band was becoming dangerously small. Too small, it seemed, for proper defense. The Red Rocks people were now practically at the mercy of the Head Splitters. In his dejection, the old chief was a pitiful sight, apparently seeing no solution.

Hump Ribs rose to the occasion. The change in his own band's status had been a heady experience for him. A taste of prosperity and the increased prestige in the Big Council had done wonders for his confidence and his leadership qualities.

"My chiefs," he began, receiving the nod of permission from Many Robes, "we have had thoughts of this matter. It would seem that the Head Splitters are attacking us more since they have elk-dogs."

Nods of agreement. He paused a moment for effect, then dropped his question into the silence of the council.

"Now why," Hump Ribs glanced around to make sure everyone was listening, "should we fear the Head Splitters? Let us get more elk-dogs, and"—he drew himself up to his tallest—"let the Head Splitters fear us!"

A cheer from his young elk-dog warriors brought stern glances from the chiefs of the other bands. This was a turning point in the history of the People. A major step, the emotional change from run-and-hide to the pride and confidence of self-sufficiency. The emergence was not a painless one. Noisy murmurs of dissension rose in the circle, and Many Robes raised a hand for silence.

"Yes, Hump Ribs," the real-chief said sternly, "go on. Where are the People to get more elk-dogs?"

Hump Ribs realized suddenly that he had overplayed his hand. He had been carried away in the excitement of the moment. Now he had no alternative but to bluff his way. He assumed an air of confidence that he did not feel, and plunged ahead.

"Where are the elk-dogs?" Hump Ribs' voice rang out. "The elk-dogs of our band came from the Head Splitters! From them we can get more."

This suggestion was met with stunned silence, then

an argumentative murmur. In all the history of the People, raids had never been planned into the country of the Head Splitters. There had been skirmishes, sometimes pitched battles, but largely of a defensive nature. The People had often showed courage, sometimes even victories. But, beyond an occasional foray, no war party had ever ventured much beyond the Red Rocks.

"Let our Elk-dog band spend the season with White Bear's people at Red Rocks," continued Hump Ribs. "Let any young men of other bands join us for a season. Our Elk-dog Society will teach them of elk-dog medicine. All the bands of the People will become mighty because of the elk-dogs."

The grandiose scheme was just improbable enough to catch the imagination of the young men. Enthusiasm mounted during the rest of the week's ceremonies. Many sacrifices were made to Sun Boy in the hope of achieving success in the coming venture.

Hump Ribs realized that the entire workability of the plan would depend on Heads Off. He drew the young man aside to enlist his co-operation.

"Come, let us talk, Heads Off," suggested the chief as they walked. "Can this thing be done?"

Garcia had been a bit irritated initially at the turn of events. After all, the elk-dog medicine was his, to teach or not, as he chose. Then, amused at himself for thinking in terms of his personal medicine, he had become interested. He was young enough and foolish enough to see the exciting possibilities of an expedition. Only a slight gnawing of conscience bothered him occasionally. After all, he was a family man, with responsibilities.

He was finally able to rationalize. The campaign to procure horses, was, actually, to make more safe and secure the lives of all the People. That would include his pregnant wife.

"Yes, my chief, we can do it," he answered.

The Red Rocks band, Garcia discovered, actually had one horse already. It was a miserable creature, found by some youngsters after the massacre. It had been either lost or abandoned by the Head Splitters. Abandoned, probably, Garcia thought as he examined the animal. The mouth was cut and bleeding from the rawhide war bridle. Raw sores were visible where ropes had chafed the animal's back and withers. Every bone was visible on the emaciated frame.

Talking with the warrior who claimed this elk-dog, Garcia found that the man was afraid of it. The misuse and neglect was not from lack of concern, but from lack of knowledge and experience. He explained the "medicine," and how the animal must be allowed to graze at least half the day. By the time the Sun Dance was over, the mistreated animal was responding well and beginning to gain weight.

The owner was one of several young men of other bands who followed Hump Ribs that season. Some of the other chiefs viewed this as a mixed blessing. They resented that their young men should follow another chief, even for a season. Still, it seemed well worthwhile to trade the temporary threat to prestige for the promise of prosperity. If the elk-dogs could only do for the other bands what they had for that of Hump Ribs! It would be a great thing for all the People.

White Bear had regained much of his proud demeanor. Here he was, leading a group twice the size of his band at its greatest. Into his own country, too. The old chief was almost wishing for a skirmish with the Head Splitters. The confidence displayed by the young elk-dog men was certainly contagious.

Garcia and his Elk-dog Society, with the various trainees from other bands, were feeling this excitement to the utmost. For most of them, this was new country. There were new sights and smells and experiences to be had. They were moving into the territory claimed by the dreaded Head Splitters.

☙ 29 ❧

THE RED ROCKS proved to be an awesome sight. Garcia was impressed beyond anything he had seen in his life. Spires like cathedrals; other masses of rock like gigantic animals. One even resembled a ship, he thought. Strange, a stone ship, observed for centuries by people who had never seen a real ship. The entire effect of the Red Rocks was that of grandeur. It was impossible to be unimpressed. For the first time Garcia could understand why the Red Rocks band continued to return to an area that had proved unkind to them. White Bear's band considered this their medicine, or that their own deity dwelt here among the magnificent Red Rocks.

Even while he marveled at the grandeur of the place,

Garcia noted problems. The topography, while ideal for the run-and-hide life-style, was also limited. The large buffalo herds of the plains would hardly come this far into the foothills. Existence would depend on enough hunting out on the plains in summer to return to the shelter of the mountains for the winter. A poor season of hunting would mean a hard winter, as only occasional deer would be available. This, in turn, had limited the size of the Red Rocks band.

This season, the People had returned early. With the combined efforts of the horsemen of the Elk-dog Society and the hunters of other bands, the kill had been great. Already the people of the Red Rocks band were enjoying more and better supplies than for many years.

The major problem at present was to hold the eager young men in check until the proper time. Instruction in elk-dog medicine had of course fallen largely to Heads Off and his Elk-dog Society. He was pleased that many of the young warriors seemed to have a natural aptitude with a horse. Of course, there were not nearly enough horses for all. Still, it was possible for each man to have a turn at instruction. The twenty-odd animals were training at least three times that number of riders.

Nothing further was seen of the Head Splitters, but a general plan emerged. An expedition to steal horses would seek out the enemy some time in the Ripening Moon. The chiefs agreed that Heads Off should lead the war party. He, in turn, would name the men to accompany him.

Garcia was pleased to have this much authority over the mission. He had been considerably worried over the possibility of an undisciplined group of enthusiastic zealots wandering over the country. Now he began to evolve a plan.

A handful of carefully chosen men would enter the enemy country on foot. There would be no use risking the horses the People already had. The six selected men, the best at elk-dog medicine, would be accompanied by Sees Far, the best scout and tracker among the People. Special care was taken to see that Sees Far could also handle and ride the elk-dogs. It might be necessary during the foray. Sees Far grumbled considerably, and his inept attempts at first were a source of great amusement. However, he saw the necessity, and in time did prove a quite adequate horseman.

In the first week of the Ripening Moon the little platoon set forth. White Buffalo had conjured up a vision which promised success, and the entire village turned out to see them off. They traveled light, but Heads Off had insisted that they carry food to avoid the necessity of stopping to hunt. Small bags of pemmican served the purpose well. In addition, each man carried a coil of light rawhide rope. They had practiced many times, by day and in darkness, once even in the rain. Any one of the elite little group could quickly tie the medicine knot around a horse's lower jaw under any conditions, within the space of a few heartbeats. Then it was a simple matter to swing up and ride.

Leaving on the journey was more difficult for Garcia than he had imagined. He and Tall One had never been apart, even a single night, since they had moved into their lodge, and the separation took on major proportions. Tall One, however, now heavy with child, seemed so filled with pride and confidence in her man that he was almost embarrassed.

Finally the journey actually began. A few thrown rocks discouraged the yapping dogs that initially tried to follow, and the war party was under way.

The general area frequented by the Head Splitters was known to be south and slightly west, so this was the direction taken. Sees Far traveled well ahead, the others following in single file. Occasionally he would ask them to wait while he spent a long while at the crest of a ridge, studying the valley ahead. Progress was slow but careful. No fires were lighted at any time.

Water became a primary problem. The country was much drier than that of the People. Sees Far proved invaluable in his ability to discover obscure game trails. Trails made by deer and elk, he pointed out, always go to water. Vegetation was of different types than those familiar to the People, also. Scrubby cedars and juniper grew on the hillsides, and in the meadows the grass seemed thin and dry by comparison with their lush prairie grasses.

At one dry camp site, the entire area was dotted with yucca and a variety of cactus. Long Elk remarked, after a chance encounter with a thorny growth, that he could now understand why the Head Splitters were so unpleasant. Anyone, beset by this terrible country, would have the temperament of an accidentally awakened bear in the Moon of Hunger. The others chuckled quietly.

There came a day when, in the clear blue of the morning air, a smudge of smoke was seen on the southern horizon. About two suns away, all agreed. It was decided to approach directly, then wait at half a day's distance while scouts moved closer to investigate. It would never do to blunder into even a small hunting party in the enemy's country with this few a number.

The group camped at a well-hidden spring, and Sees Far and Heads Off went ahead. The two took a few hours' sleep, then rose with the half moon and trotted easily in the direction of the Head Splitters' village. It was highly unlikely that any of the enemy would be out in the night. Ideally, they hoped to be overlooking the village when daylight came.

Twice Sees Far held up a hand for silence and signaled to wait. He would then disappear into the dark and be gone a few minutes. Then he would return and motion to follow.

As the pale gray of the false dawn began to show to their left, the two men smelled smoke. They crept up to the crest of the next ridge, selected an area of jumbled rock to provide hiding, and settled themselves to await daylight.

Their place of concealment directly overlooked the village. The dim shapes of the lodges could be seen spread out across the valley. Smoke drifted lazily from the smoke holes of some of the lodges. As the darkness faded, Garcia saw an encampment not unlike that of Hump Ribs. The design of the skins over the lodge doorways was slightly different, and the smoke flaps had different ornamentation. But there was the ever-present smell, and a dog yapping in the distance. A man came out of a lodge and cuffed the barking dog, who retreated, yelping. The man stretched, yawned, and walked around behind his lodge to urinate.

Sees Far touched the arm of his companion and pointed. At the far end of the valley was a grassy meadow, surrounded by hills on two sides, the rocky stream on the third, and the scattered lodges on the fourth. And, quietly grazing, lying down, or ambling slowly through the morning dampness of the grass were more horses than Garcia had ever seen at one time.

❧ 30 ☙

GARCIA stared, unbelieving. How could it be possible? He estimated nearly a hundred animals in the meadow. Where had they all come from? It could be plainly seen now that there were horses of all ages in the herd. His mind ran rapidly back over the past few years. The herd held by Hump Ribs' band had multiplied rapidly, too. He had been with the People two, no, three seasons now. The first horse they had seen had been his, and now their herd must number nearly thirty, counting foals and yearlings.

Never much interested in ciphering while in school, Garcia now painfully stirred his memory as he counted on his fingers. It had been maybe ten years since the first colonies were established in the area to the south and west. In ten years, a single mare could easily produce nine or ten foals. But, he reminded himself, half those foals would also be females. In three years, the first of those would be producing an annual offspring. That's seven more, and their foals—he gave up on the calculation, only satisfied that in a decade a few original mares could nearly populate all of New Spain.

The more pressing problem was how to steal horses from this well-protected valley. He studied the topography with the eyes of a military tactician. The only possible way to drive a herd of galloping horses at top speed would be across the stream to the east. All other directions would be too risky or impassable. A long swing to the east, then turning north, would put them on the way home to Red Rocks, able to travel rapidly. What about pursuit? He looked at the village again. Perhaps a half dozen horses were tied among the lodges. Favorite hunting horses, probably. Fast, excellent, but little threat to the rapidly moving raiding party. He touched the arm of Sees Far, and began to whisper his intended plan, pointing to landmarks as he talked.

His intention was to strike just at dawn, giving the raiders the element of surprise and the advantage of daylight for the escape. There were apparently no guards on the horse herd, so he believed that combat could be avoided entirely. It would be a swift, divisive move. Garcia chuckled to himself at the thought of the surprise to the Head Splitters. Probably nothing was further from their thoughts than invasion of their own territory by the People.

The raiding party crossed the stream a little before

the following dawn, and moved among the horses, quieting them and selecting mounts which seemed tractable. If they were discovered, a long yell would signal that all must mount and retreat or be left behind. Garcia knotted his rope around the jaw of a well-muscled young mare and swung lightly to her back. He could see other figures swinging up, dim shapes against the paling sky. He kneed the mare forward, clucking softly to the other animals. They began to drift quietly toward the stream. He encountered Long Elk, softly urging a mare with a small foal into the shallow water.

As he had hoped, the greater part of the herd trampled past the crossing, obliterating the tracks of the raiders. At least, the Head Splitters would have difficulty reading the sign. They would be unsure how many men they were following.

Apparently the clatter of hooves in the rocky bed of the stream roused some of the nearer lodges. Garcia, bringing up the rear, bent low over the horse's withers, hoping to avoid being seen. He glanced back and saw people popping like gophers out of the lodges, straining to see in the dim light. A long shout came from the village. Apparently those in the raiding party took this as the signal to retreat. Riders kicked their mounts into a run, and in a moment the entire herd was at a gallop.

It was broad daylight before the exhausted animals began to slow to a stop. Garcia called a halt to let the horses catch their wind, while he took quick stock of the situation.

The horses had followed the galloping leaders. He was sure that a few slower animals had dropped behind, but they were no great loss. In fact, thought Garcia, this may have called out the weaker individuals. Riders were calling to each other, laughing and joking at the success of the raid. Sees Far slipped away to check the back trail for pursuit.

They were well rested and nearly ready to mount up again when the scout returned.

"Heads Off, we are followed. Only two men, both riding elk-dogs." He paused, appearing confused. "I do not think they understand. They ride calmly. Can it be they do not know they were raided?"

This appeared to be the case. The very thought of attack was so foreign to the powerful Head Splitters that they apparently assumed that the horses had wandered off. Perhaps it had happened before, the animals frightened by a bear or wolves.

They watched the two riders descend the opposite slope, talking as they followed the plain trail of a hundred horses across the valley.

Suddenly Standing Bird jumped to his feet and picked up his bow.

"Go on, Heads off, I will take care of this matter." He disappeared quickly into the rocks along the back trail.

Garcia was irritated, but could see no other way out. To follow and try to stop the young man would possibly threaten the entire mission. He signaled to mount up, and the group moved out, the loose stragglers urged along by the riders.

Some time later Garcia called another rest halt. Some

of the foals were falling behind, and he wished to keep all the animals if possible. Tired colts slumped wearily to the ground, and the older animals milled around nervously, nibbling at the sparse vegetation. The riders dismounted stiffly, stamping circulation back into cramped legs.

Garcia was anxiously watching the back trail. It bothered him considerably that he had allowed young Standing Bird to turn back. Still, he had had little choice. And, viewed in perspective, he told himself irritably, the loss of one man on a mission of this sort was completely acceptable. Unfortunately, this objective view was only partially successful. Memories of the quiet smile of Standing Bird kept popping into his head. The youth had been one of the best of the horsemen. He had also developed a calm skill with his weapons that was much like that of his father, Mouse Roars. Too bad, Garcia thought, that a young man of such promise should be lost.

Sees Far pointed to the back trail.

"Heads Off, look to the notched rock just below the tree on the ridge."

Garcia strained to see, and finally made out a slight movement near the crest of the ridge.

"There are two elk-dogs," observed Sees Far. "We are still followed."

The two men watched the ridge carefully, waiting for more riders or warriors on foot to appear. None did immediately, and Garcia turned his attention to the two horsemen first observed. The animals were following the trail in single file, the leading horse picking his way daintily among the boulders of the hillside.

The rider off this horse sat with an easy, relaxed posture. A good rider, Garcia noted briefly to himself. He knows how to lean back on the downhill slope and let the horse pick his way. The other horse, he now became aware, was riderless. It was wearing a saddle or a saddle pad, but was apparently being led by the rider on the other horse. He turned his attention again to the rider. There was something familiar about the man's easy balance on the horse.

"Aiee!" Sees Far suddenly voiced a grunt of recognition. "It is Standing Bird!"

⚜ 31 ⚜

I T SEEMED a very long time that they waited while Standing Bird crossed the floor of the valley and made his way up to the group. Just as well, Garcia decided. Give the stolen horses time to quiet down and graze a little. The smaller foals were rested now, and becoming playful. Here and there a mare anxiously called, trying to locate her missing offspring. A couple of riders circled the herd, quietly keeping them from straying.

Finally Standing Bird approached, riding a black stallion and leading a likely-looking spotted mare. Their guess had been correct, Garcia noted. The very best of the horses had been the ones picketed among the lodges. Standing Bird rode into the clearing, swung a leg forward, over the horse's neck, and jumped lightly to the ground.

"We are no longer followed," he stated grimly over his shoulder as he strode toward the spring to drink.

Very little was said, but it was assumed that Standing Bird now considered his parents avenged. Long Elk pointed wordlessly to a smear of blood on the shoulder of the spotted mare.

Garcia gave the signal, and the group mounted to move on. In a short while the loose horses had adapted to being driven, and this made progress much easier.

During the next few days of easy travel, there was opportunity to observe the newly captured animals. Garcia was pleased to note that many of the horses, especially mares and foals, were of good quality. In fact, there were very few poor individuals. This seemed logical, he acknowledged to himself. Only the best horses of Europe had been selected to outfit the expeditions to New Spain. The succeeding generations would continue to maintain good quality.

He was interested in one bay mare, an older animal, apparently. A sprinkle of white hairs showed across the muzzle, indicating advanced age. She was thin, but of good substance, and nursing a fine foal. Most intriguing was a small brand on the left side of the neck. A military mark, placed there prior to boarding ship in Spain long ago. The young man felt a strange, nostalgic kinship with this old mare. Both were far from their place of origin, with no chance of return. He spent a long time stroking the glossy neck. This was a confusing situation to his companions. Why should Heads Off be so interested in this bony old elk-dog? It was Long Elk who ventured the answer.

"It has to do with the elk-dog medicine of Heads Off," he observed. "See how he looks at and touches the medicine marking on the neck."

Nods of agreement indicated that whatever the cause of the strange behavior, it was private medicine, and not to be questioned. It was also assumed that the old elk-dog was to become the property of Heads Off.

Others in the party were establishing claim to their favorite animals. Standing Bird would keep the two acquired in his private foray. After much joking, the party chose for Sees Far, a couple of quiet, dependable mares. He was still somewhat inclined to ridicule the young elk-dog men and the entire project. It was noted, however, that Sees Far did seem to take great pride in his own newly acquired elk-dogs.

Garcia, on the remainder of the journey back, became increasingly aware of another problem. A couple of the young stallions were constantly amorous toward some of the mares that showed signs of being in season. One of these was a stallion of poor quality, with large coarse head and feet. His attempted conquest was a young Andalusian mare, which distressed Garcia greatly. A mare of that quality and refinement should have only the best stallion to sire her foals. It would be necessary to plan the breeding somehow.

He was aware that in his homeland, stallions were often castrated to make them more tractable. He had seen the operation performed, and believed that this might be a solution to the present dilemma. That would allow an inferior animal, such as the jugheaded young stallion, to be useful without breeding down the quality of the herd. He was sure the operation was simple, but was a bit apprehensive about it. Could an animal bleed to death? He resolved to try it on a foal or two of lesser quality first.

Long Elk was squatting next to him, chuckling at the breeding antics of the animals. Garcia pointed out the problem, and explained his possible solution. Long Elk agreed at once.

"Of course, Heads Off. The People often remove the seed of dogs so they will be fatter for eating. It would be the same. We can do it now!"

He jumped to his feet and deftly flipped a rope around the neck of the young stallion. Long Elk was becoming very adept with the rope, Garcia noted. The horse, partially trained, respected restraint somewhat, and fought very little after the first effort.

The grooms in the stables of Garcia's father would have laughed uproariously at the ensuing scene. Working from poorly remembered observation, Garcia rigged leg ropes to throw the horse to the ground. One hind leg was drawn forward to expose the genitals. Long Elk and Garcia proceeded in an amateurish fashion, amid jokes, hoots of derision, and plentiful advice from the others.

Despite all the ineptness, the operation was successful, and the fist-sized male gonads lay in the sand when the horse scrambled to his feet. The animal did not bleed excessively. In fact, it seemed to move well and be none the worse for the experience.

Garcia was pleased, and as the journey proceeded felt increasingly optimistic about the entire elk-dog project. If the People were to use horses extensively, it would be well to have good-quality stock. His father had always insisted on using only the best of breeding stock. The People were apparently committed to ongoing conflict with the Head Splitters, who had acquired horses before and would again. It would be imperative to maintain a high quality in the herds of the People. This, he believed, could be done by selective gelding of inferior males. With proper breeding, each generation of foals would be better than the last.

Looking at the wild, undisciplined exuberance of some of his companions, Garcia had a few doubts. Could these people possibly be made to understand the long-range planning involved? Theirs had always been a hand-to-mouth existence, with little thought for the future, he believed. Still, he had encountered unexpected intelligence and thoughtfulness among the People. Coyote, his father-in-law, was certainly as clever as any man he had ever known. Hump Ribs, who increasingly reminded the young man of some of the local officials at home, was a shrewd and careful planner.

The group was now approaching the camp of the People, and a shout of triumphant welcome arose. People of all ages ran to meet them, accompanied by dozens of barking dogs. The raiders had already decided, in their unbridled enthusiasm, to create an impressive entrance by driving the horse herd directly through the village. People cheered, milled among the horses, and called to relatives and friends among the raiders.

Suddenly Garcia, with a chill of apprehension, realized that none of his family was here to greet him. Tall One, Coyote, Big Footed Woman, all were missing in the welcoming throng.

❧ 32 ❧

G ARCIA vaulted from the horse he was riding and hurried toward his lodge. What could have happened, he wondered, to prevent his wife from welcoming him back? He saw no signs that the village had been attacked, and no indication that anything was wrong. He hurried among the scattered lodges and approached his own. Outside he encountered Coyote, who, for some completely illogical reason, was wearing a broad grin. Garcia was irritated at the ridiculous good humor of his father-in-law.

"Where is my wife?" he snapped angrily. "What is wrong?"

"All is well, Heads Off. Her time is here for birthing."

Somehow that possibility had not been among the various ones that had flitted through the anxious mind of her husband. He had imagined her sick, injured, drowned, burned, or stolen, but not in labor. His irritation began to cool a little, to be replaced by anxiety. He lifted the skin and stepped through the doorway into the dim interior of the lodge.

Tall One lay on the bed, her protruding abdomen plainly visible. Big Footed Woman knelt beside her. Garcia stepped across the lodge and dropped to his knees beside the pallet, taking the girl's hand. She smiled at him, and the large dark eyes gazed into his face with the look of adoration that had always made him feel like the greatest man alive.

"You are home, my husband. Did the raid go well?"

"Yes, yes," he mumbled absently. "How is it with you?"

"It is our time." Her facial expression hardly changed as the next contraction crept in. The grasp on his hand tightened, but the dark eyes remained fixed on his face. As his vision became adjusted to the shadowy lodge, he noted a few beads of sweat on her upper lip. Nothing more. The spasm passed, and she continued in a conversational tone. "I shall bring us a fine child. Did you get many elk-dogs?"

He nodded, and she could see that he was pleased with the success of the expedition.

"You go outside now, Heads Off," interrupted Big Footed Woman. "This is a woman thing."

The young man hesitated, and the older woman put a comforting hand on his shoulder.

"All will be well. The women of our family all have easy birthing. Tall One is shaped well for it. Now," she pushed him gently, "go outside and make man-talk."

He gave Tall One's hand a last squeeze and patted her shoulder clumsily. He stumbled outside, squinting at the bright sunlight. The noise and dust of the milling horse herd drifted from the meadow beyond the lodges. Occasional exuberant shouts carried through the warm summer air.

"Come and sit, Heads Off," Coyote beckoned. The

176

back rests had been moved outside to a shady spot behind the lodges. Garcia shuffled over and sank down beside his father-in-law. He felt numb, detached from reality, his mind active yet far away. Coyote's conversational patter irritated him initially, but soon they were talking in animated excitement of the raid's success. He related the entire story, giving full credit to Standing Bird's rear-guard action. Coyote chuckled at the castration of the stallion, and asked further about this custom among the people of Heads Off.

Even with the distraction of conversation, time dragged slowly. Once Big Footed Woman stepped from the lodge and Garcia scrambled to his feet. The woman motioned him to be seated again, and called to one of her children to go fetch a skin of water. She disappeared again, and time dragged slowly on. Sun Boy's torch was low in the sky when at last it happened.

Even after the endless waiting, Garcia was hardly emotionally prepared when a thin, choking cry was heard from the lodge. It was followed by a moist cough and then a full-throated squall. A bellow, almost, Coyote said later. Both men were standing at the lodge door almost instantly. In a short while Big Footed Woman lifted the skin of the doorway and beckoned them inside.

Tall One lay holding a fur-wrapped infant in the crook of her arm. The bulge of her abdomen was now flat again. Garcia still felt numb, light-headed, and a little confused. Tall One lifted a corner of the fur, and the baby's big dark eyes blinked at the fading light of day.

"You have a son, Heads Off," she said proudly. The girl appeared tired, but happy, and a trifle concerned. Perhaps a bit too concerned, he realized with apprehension. He turned to look at Big Footed Woman, and saw it in her face, also. A touch of sadness, regret, and worry. Something, he saw, was wrong with the baby.

"What is it?" Silence. "What is it?" Only the sad looks of regret from both women. He looked to his wife and she turned her face from him, tears starting from under the long lashes. She felt she had failed him, he realized.

This was a totally unexpected turn of events. He had been concerned throughout the pregnancy, but all his concern had been for his wife. It had never occurred to him that the child might have some defect, some deformity. He knew such things did happen, but in his youth and inexperience, he had always expected them to happen to others. Now, apparently, tragedy had occurred to him and Tall One.

He had no inkling of how severe the deformity might be. The child was completely enveloped in soft furs, and he could see only the face. The bright eyes and chubby cheeks appeared healthy enough. The facial features were even and attractive. It must be with the arms or legs. A club foot, perhaps.

Garcia's regrets were directed toward the disappointment his wife must feel. What a heartbreak to think of the agile, athletic Tall One, raising a crippled child. He must know the extent of the deformity. With tears starting in his eyes, he turned to Big Footed Woman.

"You must tell me, Mother," he mumbled, head

swimming in numb confusion. "What is wrong with the child?"

Big Footed Woman turned to him sadly, and a tear rolled down her cheek.

"It is nothing, Heads Off," she began. "It is only that Tall One and I are so saddened. We had hoped that the son of Heads Off might have fur upon the face also, like the father's."

The relief was like a plunge in cold water. Garcia sat down on the floor of the lodge and began to laugh.

"You mean, that is the problem? That the face has no fur?" He collapsed in laughter again. No one else was laughing, except for a nervous giggle from Coyote. They obviously did not understand and, in fact, were beginning to be a bit irritated. He paused for breath.

"That comes much later, Mother," he explained. The others looked puzzled. He reached across and unfolded the fur of the infant's wrappings, exposing the well-formed little body.

"See? There is no fur upon the private parts, either! That comes later!"

Understanding flooded across the faces of the others, and the laughter started. In a moment, tears of relief were flowing as they hugged each other. The noise of their excitement carried outside and someone called to question whether all was well with the lodge of Heads Off. Coyote stepped outside.

"Heads Off has a son!" he announced loudly. Children scattered to carry the word, and in a few minutes the entire band would know the exciting news. Coyote re-entered the lodge to look again at his grandson. Tall

One had put the infant to breast, and he was responding eagerly.

"I will call the child Many Elk-dogs," she murmured proudly, "to honor the deeds of his father against the Head Splitters."

∿ 33 ≥

OTHER HONORS were in the offing for the raiding party. The People were already starting a victory celebration, the like of which had never been seen. Many dogs were killed, much meat was cooked, of all sorts, and the dancing and celebration lasted for three days.

At the end of that time the People moved the camp. It seemed a prudent thing to do, since the Head Splitters would be looking for revenge. There were some older members among the Red Rocks band who felt that they should winter in the traditional area. Better judgment prevailed, however. Most people recognized the greater safety of some sheltered meadow farther out on the prairie.

Besides, it was becoming apparent that the large horse herd would present a big factor in selecting camp sites. They must choose an area with adequate graze.

A good camp site was chosen on the south bank of a heavily timbered stream, and the People began to make preparations for winter. Already the chill of the prairie nights foretold the first frosts of the Moon of Falling Leaves. Long lines of geese honked their way south, and the purple and gold of the autumn flowers gave way to the changing colors of the prairie. The sumacs flared a brilliant red for a few days and then dropped their leaves for the season.

There was no hunting to be done. Supplies were more than adequate. The People were enjoying the luxury of having been able to secure enough buffalo in advance to winter well. The elk-dogs were making great changes in the People's way of life.

With more time available, and the plentiful supply of skins for dwellings, several families began to construct new lodges. It was during this season that another change in the customs of the People began to be apparent. Previously, the size of a lodge was limited. It must be moved by dogs, or by people, and the weight of the lodge cover could not be too heavy to transport. Now, there seemed no limit to the loads an elk-dog could transport with a drag. As a consequence, the new dwellings were larger. Lodges of twenty or more buffalo skins became commonplace. Without the elk-dogs, a lodge cover of this size could not have been transported.

Hump Ribs, although his lodge was relatively new, felt obliged to acquire a new one. It would never do for the chief to have a smaller lodge than those of other members of the band. The wives of Hump Ribs were, as a group, experts at dressing and tanning skins. The new lodge was a beautiful thing to look at, the soft cover decorated with designs of the buffalo, medicine animal of the chief.

Hump Ribs, with all his wives and children, moved into the new lodge well before the first snows. Of course, there were those women who insisted they would not want such a big lodge. Think of the wood and buffalo chips required to heat such a dwelling, they told each other. It was noted with amusement that these grumblers were usually the wives of ne'er-do-wells, who would probably never afford a fine lodge anyway.

Tall One's name for the baby did not stick. Big Footed Woman referred to the child as "Hairless One" in an amused manner recalling her concern. Coyote went a step further, and proudly referred to the "Bald Eagle," or sometimes even the "Buzzard," after that carrion eater's featherless head and neck. Others among the People referred to the "Child of Heads Off," or simply "Little Heads Off." To Garcia, "Many Elk-dogs," the mother's choice, was not his favorite name. Still, he felt irritably, there should be some semblance of order in naming the child. He was appalled that everyone simply called the baby whatever he wished, in a careless, joking manner. He spoke of this to his wife one evening as they settled down for the night. Tall One laughed.

"It is no matter, my husband. The child does not keep these names anyway. They are only used until the naming at the time of First Dance."

"I do not understand. When is the First Dance?"

"Aiee, Heads Off! Sometimes you learn nothing. Remember when the very small of the Rabbit Society go to the dance in their second summer? They are named then."

"It is well, then. What shall we name the child when it goes to First Dance?"

"No, no, Heads Off. The parents do not name the child. It is named by the Uncle."

Here the dialogue broke down with a language problem. The term used by Tall One was a word he had heard used to refer to cousins, uncles, grandfathers, or close friends of a family. Coyote had even used it in reference to White Buffalo, the medicine man. Apparently it was a loosely applied term used to indicate almost any male relative or respected friend.

"And who might the 'Uncle' be, Mother of my child?" he teased her.

"My father, Coyote, of course. It is always the oldest man of a family. Coyote will choose the name."

There were still many things to understand, Garcia mused, shaking his head.

"And what will the child be called?"

She shook her head again. "It must not be told. The People learn how the child is to be called at First Dance! No one knows until then but the Uncle. Coyote will probably," she mused, "give his own name."

That was the usual custom, the girl continued. "It is important to give away one's name before one dies. Then the name does not die." This avoided speaking the name of the dead, she said, which would be very bad medicine.

What a strange custom, he thought. I will not even know my son's name until his second summer, and then I have no choice in the matter.

"Of course," Tall One was continuing, "that name is only used until the child becomes a man. Then the name may be kept or a new one chosen, as the young man wishes."

She turned the softness of her body and snuggled warmly against her husband. He still felt very confused. It might be years, he decided, before he would even know his own son's name! Oh, well, he could worry about that later. Meanwhile, there were far nicer things to think about just now. He took her in his arms, and breathed softly in her ear.

ꙮ 34 ꙮ

THE SUN DANCE the following year was a memorable one. Even the old people could remember no time of such joy and feasting. The sacrifices of thanksgiving would be many and of high quality. Each of the bands now possessed enough elk-dogs to make hunting easier. The younger elements of the Red Rocks band had seen the wisdom of moving out onto the prairie, and this approach now prevailed.

As the various bands began to gather, the Elk-dog band of Hump Ribs was the acknowledged leader of the new progressive movement. They had had elk-dogs first and had more knowledge of elk-dog medicine. The medicine, it was said, had been brought by the strange, hair-faced Heads Off from a far tribe. Now, the stranger had married one of the most beautiful of the women of the Elk-dog band. In fact, there was a child, a son. The more curious and inquisitive tried hard to get a good look at the child. There must be something different about its appearance. To their disappointment, it appeared much like any other healthy child of the People.

There were rumors among some of the other bands that the son of Heads Off had been born with a full set of teeth, and that he had small horns, cleverly concealed in the hair. There were even those who whispered that perhaps the child was not from the loins of the hair-faced stranger at all. After all, there was no fur upon the face, and the appearance did not seem unusual.

Others were inclined to ridicule the entire substance of rumor and doubt. Was it not true that Heads Off was a respected warrior of the Elk-dog band? Was he not said to be a skilled hunter and a brave fighter in combat against the Head Splitters? Such a man deserved respect, regardless of fur upon the face. Some of the People, it was noted, had more facial hair than others. If he chose not to pluck the thick fur, who could blame him? Aiee, that would be painful! Perhaps in some way the facial fur related to the beliefs of the stranger's people or to his medicine. And that, as all could plainly see, was powerful.

Garcia had attempted to conform to the customs of the People. To please his wife, as much as any other reason. If Tall One was happy, he found himself happy, also. When he had first joined the People, he had been a bit slipshod about his appearance. When his hair and beard grew too long, he had hacked off a portion with his belt knife. Now, since his marriage, Tall One had assumed a responsibility for the care of his hair and beard. She had begun by playfully braiding his hair into the unique style of the People. Her husband did not object and, in fact, enjoyed the closeness of physical contact. The grooming sessions had usually deteriorated into a very physical romp on the robes of the bed.

Now, he had begun to see that it was important to her for him to make an impressive appearance. He had long since become comfortable in the buckskin leggings and breechclout. The moccasins, with hard rawhide soles and soft tanned uppers, were the most practical foot gear he had ever used. He had noted with pleasure that his own garments were of better workmanship than many of the others. This spoke well for the competence of the women of Coyote's family. The quill embroidery of Big Footed Woman was the finest of any in Hump Ribs' band. His daughter, Tall One, had inherited the aptitude, and some said, was already doing handiwork as fine as that of her mother.

Of course, the wives of Heads Off and Coyote had the best of materials to work with. The skill of Heads Off in the hunting of buffalo with the elk-dog and the real-spear had become legendary. He was respected all the more for his willingness to teach his elk-dog medicine to the young men of the People.

As her husband rose in prestige among the tribe, Tall One was anxious that he be well dressed and well groomed. He had consented easily to allow his hair to grow, and it had now become long enough to braid properly. He was a warrior even more handsome than she had thought at first, she decided. The beard was still a source of wonder to her. That a man would have fur upon his face was a curious thing. Not that she objected. The furry face did tickle against her neck and her ear lobe sometimes at night, but this was a deliciously exciting sensation. The beard was more like a talisman or identifying mark for her husband. She had come to think of it as a mark of distinction. Perhaps that was why she had felt so strongly, wishing that the child would share that physical sign. A sign of royal blood, in effect, the mark of aristocracy. She could now hardly wait until the baby grew to manhood to see if he inherited the trait.

"Do not wish time away," her mother had advised her, but still, it would be so important to see if her son's face would bear fur. She sighed and gently touched the cradle board, propped against a back rest. The baby gurgled and laughed. He was developing so rapidly, she thought. I will not have a baby but a short while. He will soon be a child.

The infant had a striking personality for one so young. From the first, his bright and inquiring eyes had missed nothing. He smiled easily, and seemed to have the humor of his grandfather, the Coyote. He was already making small talking noises in an attempt to communicate. And all this in less than six moons! This was obviously, Tall One told herself, a superior child. She was flattered, although sometimes a trifle annoyed, by all the attention that the son of Heads Off was attracting at the Sun Dance. All in all, hers was a happy and exciting life.

Coyote and Heads Off approached and entered the lodge, talking earnestly. They hardly spoke to her, and she saw that her husband seemed more concerned than usual. Her father, characteristically, seemed to be doing more listening than talking. She quickly gathered the drift of the conversation. A few of the young warriors, intoxicated with the success of the horse-stealing raid, were making war talk. A full-scale invasion would punish the Head Splitters in their own country.

"This must not be!" Heads Off was insisting. "We are not ready. They will throw away all we have gained!"

He could hardly believe how rapidly the attitudes of the People had changed. It seemed only a short while ago that he had had difficulty in persuading Hump Ribs' band to even pursue the abductors of their children. Their entire thinking had been defensive, avoiding of conflict. True, most of the oldsters still felt this way. But success had been an exciting thing for the young men. They had experienced successful forays against the dreaded traditional enemy. Forgotten already was the fact that the successes had been due to careful planning.

"The elk-dogs bring mixed problems," observed Coyote finally. "Before, the young men were kept busy hunting enough meat to keep hunger away. Now, hunting is easier, and they have more time to think of other things."

Garcia agreed, but regardless of the cause, he could foresee trouble. Where previously he had almost despaired of inciting the People to fight even in their own defense, his problem was now almost the opposite. The young men with their new-found skills must be prevented from riding out in small groups, looking for trouble. They would be sure to find it. More importantly, perhaps, such actions would risk the loss of the valuable horses. Garcia's formal military training still made itself felt.

"Never mind for now," Coyote was saying. He rose to make his way out of the lodge. "It will be talked of tonight at the Big Council."

ࣶ 35 ࣶ

THE BIG COUNCIL of the previous year had seemed tense with excitement, but that was all eclipsed by this one. It seemed that no one wanted to miss any of the proceedings. More of the women were in attendance than usual, standing around the periphery of the formal circle to catch every word of the council talk.

The big news was, of course, known to all. This past season would be remembered for many generations as the Year of Elk-dogs. It remained only for Hump Ribs to make a formal report to the Council.

One of the other chiefs had a story, also, of comparatively lesser importance. Garcia thought, however, that it might ultimately prove of equal meaning to the People.

"I am Black Beaver, chief of the Mountain band of the People. We have wintered well, at the Big Timbers, and we have seen the Head Splitters." A murmur in the circle told that this news had not been heard by all present. "We met them as we came to the Sun Dance.

They had wives and children, as we did, so there was no fighting. But, they are very angry."

An amused chuckle came from the circle, finally silenced by a hand gesture from Many Robes.

"They were very bitter about the loss of their elk-dogs," Black Beaver continued. "They had only a few with them. But they also said that their real-chief, Gray Wolf, is still in a rage over the death of his son. He has sworn to kill Heads Off, who is called Hair Face among them. And they made many threats against the People."

There were hoots of derision from some of the younger warriors, but many of the oldsters looked very grim. The threats of Head Splitters were not to be taken lightly. Garcia resolved to ask more about the real-chief, who had once again threatened his life.

At last came the time of the Elk-dog band to speak.

"I am Hump Ribs, chief of the Elk-dog band of the People," he began. His confidence had expanded with his prestige and he was an imposing figure. He was now one of the most respected of the chiefs. There were some who were beginning to speak of Hump Ribs as possibly the next real-chief. Old Many Robes had seen many winters, and at the time of his passing, the chiefs of all the bands would select one of their number to take his place. What better man than the leader of the Elk-dog band, the once insignificant group that had now come to such prominence in the tribe?

Hump Ribs was not unaware of these rumors, and he reveled in the speculation. His report in Council, then, must be worthy of a potential real-chief. He was a good storyteller, and managed to milk the utmost in suspense and excitement out of the story of the raid. Of course, his listeners had already heard the story. This only made it more delicious in the retelling.

The story was so inspiring that the excitement began to mount, and by the time Hump Ribs finished, a group of young warriors at the rear were shouting inflammatory remarks.

"Teach the Head Splitters a lesson!"

"Show them we are the People!"

"Death to the Head Splitters!"

The group was not easily quieted, but finally order prevailed. There was brief discussion among the chiefs, all of whom were in agreement. The time was not right for a move against the enemy. Old Many Robes spoke very firmly, directly to the younger element in the rear. Such a foray was forbidden. They nodded glumly, and remained quiet.

Garcia could see the moody look of insurrection in the faces of the youths. It was plain that they had no confidence in the leadership of the aging Many Robes. He could not be expected, they would be thinking, to understand the intricacies of the new elk-dog thing. The situation was ripe for problems of a very serious nature.

Of one thing, Garcia was pleased. The dissenters were primarily not of Hump Ribs' band. It gave him some degree of pride that most of his Elk-dog Society were possessed of better discipline.

After the Council adjourned, he walked away toward

the lodges with his father-in-law.

"Coyote, twice now there have been threats on my life from this Head Splitter chief. Tell me more of this man."

"I know very little, Heads Off. One does not become very familiar with Head Splitters." He paused to giggle nervously. "I have seen Gray Wolf a time or two. A big, powerful man, said to be a fierce fighter, and has honors from many victories. Never has there been so young a real-chief among them. Gray Wolf has no more than forty winters. It is too bad that you have killed his favorite son, for this man is a powerful enemy."

It was a long speech for Coyote, and full of important information. For the first time, Garcia began to realize the seriousness of the threats. Somehow he had envisioned the Head Splitter chief as an old man, like Many Robes. That would be no physical threat. But here was news of a vow made by an expert warrior, hardly past his prime. Apparently the Head Splitter had placed all the misfortunes of his tribe squarely on the shoulders of one young hair-faced warrior. And not too incorrectly, Garcia supposed. He could see two events as inevitable. One, an all-out pitched battle between the two tribes, and the other a personal combat to the death between himself and the real-chief of the Head Splitters. He was mildly concerned over the latter, but had confidence in his own training and ability.

More worrisome was the other likelihood. The constant threat was that some of the young dissenters would bring on a conflict prematurely. Confident as the young men were, they had only a few moons' experience with their elk-dogs. Some of them were very proficient at hunting, to be sure. But, there was a great deal of difference between a run with the lance at a fleeing bison, and a charge at another charging horseman whose every desire is to kill you. He was afraid that the eager younger men would find themselves in combat beyond their abilities. Combat that would endanger the rest of the People.

His worst fears were realized a few days later at the end of the Sun Dance. As Hump Ribs' band moved out, it was discovered that one of the young men was missing. Inquiry revealed another absent from the Red Rocks band, and two more from the Mountain band. All, it appeared, had been among the grumblers at the Big Council.

They had apparently stolen silently away in the night. Each had ridden his elk-dog, and each had taken all the weapons he possessed.

≈ 36 ≈

THERE WAS little to be done. The four dissenters had told no one their plans. It was assumed that they had undertaken a personal vendetta against the enemy. Some people told the families of the missing youths that they had probably gone on a private hunting trip, but no one seriously believed it.

Plans continued for the breaking of camp, and the chiefs led their bands in various directions for the summer. Hump Ribs' band moved southeasterly, into the Tall Grass country. This was the most pleasant, to Garcia, of the diverse sorts of terrain he had seen since he had been with the People.

On the third day of travel, Sees Far, scouting ahead, found the trail of four elk-dogs, traveling together. He came back to report, and extra precautions were taken to establish security. It seemed likely that the four horses were ridden by the missing youths, but with all the changes taking place on the prairie, there was no way to be sure. There could have been other elk-dogs. It was hoped that the young men, knowing the general area selected for the summer's activities, had simply gone on ahead to hunt.

Garcia did not believe this. He had seen the defiant looks at the Big Council, and was certain that this was a rebellious gesture. These were young men deliberately defying the authority of the chiefs. They could easily be in considerably more trouble than they could handle, he was afraid.

Two Hawks, the one youth from his own band, had been a headstrong, difficult individual. He was sullen and resentful of any offered help. Garcia had often wondered why he bothered to attend the learning sessions. Apparently the youth had now found kindred spirits in the other bands.

The four horsemen were obviously equipped to travel much more rapidly than the rest of the band. Their tracks became more difficult to follow as the distance between the groups increased. A few suns later, after a light summer rain, the trail was obliterated entirely. Concern for the young men persisted, although there were some who were inclined to shrug the entire incident away. Such irresponsible behavior deserved any misfortune that might befall them, declared one old woman.

Apprehension was heightened somewhat by the discovery of the trail of another large band of people. The trail was several suns old, and the tracks included those of elk-dogs. There were also grooves made by the dragging of many lodge poles.

Since it was known that none other of the People were in this area, this must be a band from another tribe. They could not be the Growers. The Growers did not use skin lodges, but log-and-mud dwellings, and therefore would not be dragging lodge poles. There were other tribes of semi-hunters, but again, their lodges were made of grass thatch, and were permanently placed.

Farther north, Coyote told his son-in-law, other tribes used lodges of this sort. But here, in the area of the Tall Grass Hills, it seemed that the likeliest possibility was the most dreaded one. The trail was very probably made by Head Splitters. This theory was supported by a find next day. A pair of cast-off moccasins had been left at the camp site of the band whose trail they had encountered. The worn-out foot gear were plainly of the pattern preferred by the Head Splitters.

There was some small comfort in the apparent fact that this was a band of family units. As Garcia had noticed before, conflict was avoided at all costs when the fighting might involve the tribe's own women and children. Thus, there was frequent contact between the

Head Splitters and the People without actual combat. The risk from the enemy lay in the possibility of encountering a war party. A few mounted and armed Head Splitters would be much more of a threat than an entire band, such as the one that had made this trail.

Nevertheless, security was tightened and sentries were posted at night. Garcia took his turn at sentry duty, like the other warriors. There was a certain degree of pride in so complete an acceptance by his wife's people.

Besides, he rather enjoyed night watch. He had as a cadet, when assigned night guard duty at the academy. It was a private time to think, alone in the stillness of night. Strange, he thought, looking out over the moonlit prairie. That seemed so long ago, and worlds distant. The smells of the night were different, too. The orange blossoms and jasmine had been replaced by the spicy scent of prairie blossoms whose names he did not even know. At least, he mused, by their names in any but the language of the People.

The night sounds of the prairie were a constant interest to him, too. He smiled at the distant coyote song, recalling the evening of his first communication with Coyote, now his father-in-law. Closer at hand, a fox yapped in the gully. He identified the call of Kookooskoos, the great owl, and the soft whirring trill of the little owl. Another bird call came from the timber by the creek. He recalled that though he had heard the eerie call of this night bird many times, he had never seen the creature. Strange, how so many creatures of the prairie seemed invisible unless one really concentrated on the fact of their existence. This was part of the People's awareness of the living things all around them. He wondered if, before he knew the People, he would even have been aware of the sounds of the frogs along the creek, or the night insects among the grass.

The sky began to pale, and the People began to stir. Garcia watched Sun Boy climb over the rim of the world, and then rejoined his family to prepare for the day's journey.

By midmorning, the chill of the prairie night had given way to the day's heat. This was perhaps the warmest day of the season. There was no breeze, and the rising air currents were proving ideal for a pair of buzzards soaring high above the next hill. Garcia, as he rode, watched the birds in their endless circling. It was remarkable, he had many times thought, how long the birds could remain aloft without apparently moving a wing.

Another buzzard appeared beyond the hill, and then as they topped a small rise, he could see others. Maybe a dozen birds in all, circling, turning, the center of their attention in the area just beyond the ridge. Garcia began to wonder what was attracting the attention of so many scavengers. A buffalo carcass, perhaps?

Another uneasy thought suddenly crept into the back of his mind. It had barely had time to form any substance, when Sees Far, scouting in front of the column, came trotting back from where he had looked over the crest of the ridge. It was obvious from his manner that the scout was carrying news of great importance.

The People knew already the grim news that Sees Far carried. He trotted back toward the column part way, then stopped, made the sign for mourning, and beckoned them forward.

The four bloating bodies lay directly in the trail. They had been arranged there deliberately, in a row, in a flaunting manner. Flies buzzed or crawled around and over wounds and over sightless eyes. All clothing and weapons had been removed.

Two of the young men had multiple wounds, indicating that they had died fighting. The other two bodies had the hands tied. They had been captured and tortured, it appeared. There were burns, as if from burning brands, on the skin. All four heads were crushed by the blow of a stone war club. There was no doubt that the vengeful Head Splitters wished their identity clearly known.

The mother of Two Hawks began the eerie, high-pitched wail of the mourning song, and others joined in. There was little consolation in the fact that Two Hawks had been one of those who had gone down fighting. Preparations were made for the scaffold burial in the trees along the stream, and the ceremonies were carried out rapidly. The intensity of the summer heat required rapid disposition of the bodies.

The pretty little creek, splashing in inviting coolness over white gravel shallows and plunging into deep crystal pools, received a new name. Formerly called Sycamore Creek, it would be from that day known to the People as Head Split Creek.

The men of the People, while mourning the deaths,

were also concerned with the loss of the horses. The loss of four of the People's best elk-dogs was not to be taken lightly. Despite the stark tragedy of the scene by the creek, Garcia was irritated and angry. The inconsiderate actions of the young men did not affect only themselves. They had placed the entire band in jeopardy by risking, and ultimately losing, four warriors and four elk-dogs. Such a reduction in fighting strength could be serious. In fact, four warriors, in an all-out battle, could easily make the difference in victory or defeat.

One thing seemed certain now. Eventually, there must be an all-out battle. The challenge of the Head Splitters was clear. The flaunting execution of the four young men was an open invitation to war.

Hump Ribs called council at the evening camp. There were a few hotheads who demanded bloody retribution, but a calmer approach ultimately prevailed. The Head Splitters, Coyote pointed out, would expect pursuit. They could easily ambush a war party, from a selected position of their own choosing. Why give them that advantage?

The eventual decision was to change the direction of travel slightly to avoid the enemy band this season. The time could be spent to good advantage in perfecting the skills of weaponry and use of the elk-dogs. The greater ease of hunting would allow more leisure for practice of the warrior skills. Then, by the time—whenever it might come—for combat with the Head Splitters, the People would be ready.

Despite the initial shock and tragedy that began the

season, it proved a pleasant and profitable one. There were many small elk-dogs. The castration of the colts of less desirable quality was becoming common. Several of the young men were becoming almost as proficient with the elk-dogs as Heads Off himself. The morale of the Elk-dog Society continued high, and the urgency to do something spectacular had abated somewhat. The scene on Head Split Creek had been a sobering experience for those who might otherwise have been troublemakers. The value of cautious planning had been very forcibly demonstrated.

It was a good grass year. Not only did the elk-dogs do well, but game was plentiful. The buffalo were fat and numerous. The People had a prosperous season, and when they moved southward into winter camp, they were well-fed, happy, and confident. The traditional dances in the Falling Leaves Moon expressed a large measure of thankfulness and optimism.

Garcia was more observant of the First Dance ceremony this season. Next year would be the naming ceremony for his own son. Slowly, he had begun to grasp the logic of the People's naming customs. At first, a child is called by his parents, who have complete responsibility for his survival. Next, the child meets his expanded family, headed by his Uncle. This "family" unit included pretty much the entire band, Garcia had concluded. He was constantly more impressed with the manner in which everyone took responsibility for the instruction, even the safety, of all the children, not just their own. Children were an important part of the life of the People, he realized.

More so, perhaps, than in his own culture.

So, it was logical, he decided, that the child's name would come from outside the immediate lodge for this period of years. Symbolically, it was the acceptance of the child by the tribe.

The name change at manhood was something else, again. Juan had never particularly admired his given name. He had never really known anyone who did like his own name, he recalled. How very logical to allow a person to select his own name when he proved himself, he thought. A man could be anything he fancied himself, if he had the competence to achieve it.

He had noticed that it was not always completely predictable. One young man, who thought himself somewhat more proficient than he really was, attempted to adopt the name "the Bowman." He had managed a lucky shot on his first buffalo hunt, and was forever retelling the story. The People, with great insight, persisted in ignoring the young man's choice. They called him "the Magpie," after the noisy black and white bird. The more the young man voiced protest against this nickname, the more appropriate it became. The final result was that he was forced, although gently, to stop his boasting. He must concentrate on really earning a name that would befit a capable hunter and warrior.

Sometimes a nickname of this sort would become permanent, however. The name of Coyote had begun as a joking description of his laugh. And Garcia's own name, Heads Off, had begun as a joke. Now, after the intervening years, he thought of himself almost exclusively as Heads Off.

All in all, he finally decided, it was a reasonable custom. A person's name often provided much information about him. He thought of Mouse Roars. How appropriately descriptive the name had been. A quiet man, looking almost like a mouse, but whose deeds had roared. The People could certainly use a man of those abilities now, Garcia thought with regret. The coming seasons would be critical ones for the People.

❧ 37 ❧

COYOTE did not give the child of Heads Off and Tall One his own name. To the surprise of everyone, he departed from the expected and called the boy simply "Eagle." Coyote made a short speech at the naming ceremony at First Dance.

"This one was born without fur," he began, producing chuckles around the circle. "This one has been called by some the 'Bald Eagle.' There is now hair, at least upon the head, but the eyes of this one are bright and far seeing. Let the flight of this child be high and far. Let his name be called 'the Eagle.'"

Garcia was pleased by this choice. The child had been a favorite of the entire band as he grew. Bright, alert, with the quick wit of his grandfather, the Coyote. His smile and his ready laugh made the infant a pleasure to be around. Coyote's reference to his far-seeing eyes was not an idle reference. It had been noticed almost since the child's birth that his eyes were wide with wonder. The round little face seemed to have an expression of age and understanding, like the eyes of a little old man in the body of an infant.

The infant's body had developed rapidly, also. During the two years since his birth, all the children of People had been exceedingly well fed. In fact, there were jokes that the Moon of Hunger needed a new name. There had been little hunger, for meat was plentiful with the changing of the hunting methods.

The youths now grew to manhood expecting to be initiated into the intricacies of elk-dog medicine. Of course, most of the children now had ridden horses while growing up. Eagle himself, before he could walk, had been allowed to sit on Lolita's gray withers. In fact, his mother, Tall One, had occasionally tied him to the little mare's back for a period of time. The baby laughed and gurgled happily, or dozed in the sun, while the mare grazed. The rocking motion as the animal moved was a comforting sensation, and the busy hands of Tall One were freed for her endless household tasks. Other young mothers followed suit, and the next generation of the People were soon almost literally growing up on horseback.

Hump Ribs' band had had no contact at all with the Head Splitters since the incident at Head Split Creek the previous year. Some cautiously said that perhaps the enemy had vacated the area entirely. This seemed not the case, however. Other bands had reported at the Big Council, chance meetings without conflict. There were again the veiled threats by the enemy. There had been mention of the four young men who had been foolish enough to follow the Head Splitters, and of their fate. And, at each contact, there was mention by the enemy of Heads Off, the Hair Face. Their chief still brooded with vengeance over the loss of his son. Surely, when the expected major attack came, it would be directed at the Elk-dog band.

Garcia was of the opinion that the Head Splitters were building strength, probably obtaining more elk-dogs from their Spanish contacts to the southwest. He agreed that the strike, when it came, would be against Hump Ribs' band. He felt with regret that he might be responsible for this threat. And yet, what band was capable of repelling attack more successfully? The young men were well armed, well mounted, and trained to a skilled degree. The Elk-dog band of Hump Ribs was now easily the most respected band of the People. Hump Ribs had not only grown in prestige, but also in leadership ability. Garcia had increasing respect for the judgment of the chief. Some men, he noted, become considerably better leaders under the pressures of responsibility. There was increasing certainty that Hump Ribs would be the next real-chief.

It was in the Greening Moon that the attack came. Garcia had noticed that previous attacks on the People by the Head Splitters were in the springtime. The young men of the enemy would be restless after the confinement of the winter. There would be forays out onto the plains to hunt or, if opportunity offered, to raid against the People. Therefore, it came as no surprise that the enemy chose this time of year for the attack.

The People, by long custom, had scouts out in all directions looking for the return of the buffalo. The dry grass had been fired, and the hills were greening with new growth. Scouts had been instructed to range no more than two suns away from the village, and to report back at regular intervals. Long Elk and Standing Bird, scouting to the northwest, first observed the enemy war party.

The Head Splitters were no more than two days' distance, traveling cautiously and casting about for signs of the People. All were mounted, well armed, and they were over fifty in number. The two young men remained hidden. Long Elk stayed to observe while the other carried the news of the invasion. From this time forward, the enemy was under close observation at all times.

The defense of the People depended largely on the topography of the area. Winter camp had been established in an easily defensible meadow. The valley was long and narrow. The stream on the south and a rough, rocky hillside running parallel to it on the north bordered a flat, grass strip several hundred paces wide. Near the center of this strip was the camp itself. East of the lodges, enclosed by even rougher stone outcroppings, was the sheltered meadow used to hold the horse herd.

The only direction from which an attack could come was from the west. At that end, the valley opened to a broad, flat prairie, ideal for an approach by horsemen. Up this valley would come the charge.

By this time it was assumed that the camp of the Elk-dog band was under observation by scouts of the enemy. A carefully contrived charade was carried out to make everything appear normal. Women scraped skins and chattered to each other at their work. Men lounged against their back rests and visited, and children played happily among the lodges. To the enemy they must appear totally unsuspecting.

The horse herd had been carefully divided. Mares, foals, and immature animals were herded into the meadow behind the lodges, openly watched over by youths too young for combat. The best of the hunting horses, meanwhile, were kept hidden in the heavy timber along the creek, each under the care of its owner. White Buffalo's vision promised success in the venture.

Part of the strategy involved enticing the enemy to attack at the proper moment. A decoy hunting party set out next morning in an innocent manner. Four young men, mounted on the fastest and most surefooted of horses, set out casually, wandering as if looking for game. They were sure to be observed, and avoided any opportunity for surprise or ambush by using the terrain. Finally, at the proper location, they showed themselves at the top of the hill, and pretended panic at the discovery of the enemy.

They turned and urged their horses in frantic escape. The Head Splitters, scenting blood, raced in hot pursuit. The four youths pounded across the valley, down the long strip of meadow, and in among the lodges, screaming the warning.

Behind them came the rolling thunder of dozens of hooves. Women screamed, children scurried, and there was a general exodus from the village as the People fled in panic before the charge. Echoing down the valley and re-echoing from the rocky hillside, came the chilling war cry of the Head Splitters.

❧ 38 ❧

TO THE CHARGING HEAD SPLITTERS, this must have seemed an ideal raid. To be able to pursue four terrified youths directly into the unprotected camp of the enemy was beyond all expectations. People were screaming and running frantically away from the attack, toward the timber beyond the horse meadow.

The first of the riders had almost reached the nearest of the lodges when the unexpected happened. From behind and within the front row of scattered lodges, suddenly appeared well-armed warriors. The seasoned bowmen of the band, led by Hump Ribs himself, loosed a flight of arrows at almost point-blank range. The effect was devastating. Several riders were swept from their mounts, and horses in the front ranks went down before the withering fire. The charge faltered, then re-formed for another approach, just in time to be met with another barrage of arrows. Casualties were heavy again.

The horsemen milled in confusion, attempting to reorganize, under the shouted commands of their chief. Just at that moment came a long yell from the timber. Dozens of young warriors of the Elk-dog Society poured out of the trees with lances ready, cutting off the avenue of retreat for the enemy. A few of the Head

Splitters fled in panic into the broken rocks of the hillside. Others turned to meet the new attack, and in the space of a few heartbeats, the two groups of horsemen were mixed in a dusty, bloody melee.

The Head Splitters were traditionally fierce fighters, skilled in the use of weapons. In addition, they were fighting for survival, trapped between the foot soldiers of Hump Ribs and the mounted lancers of Heads Off. There was no retreat, and the invading force fought with the ferocity of a trapped cougar at bay.

The men of the People, although backed by a tradition of defensive combat only, had readied for this day. The pent-up resentment of years, perhaps centuries of abuse by the Head Splitters, was reaching its climax today. Lances found human torsos as vulnerable as the rib cages of buffalo, and warriors tumbled into the dust.

Garcia kneed his mare, Lolita, through the milling, fighting crowd, searching for the Head Splitter chief. He made a run with the lance at a youth hardly older than Long Elk. The young warrior initially made a firm stand, readying his shield and club. At the last moment, his resolve faltered, and he threw himself backward from his horse to avoid the lance thrust. Garcia swept past, unable to stop his charge, and as he glanced down, saw the young Head Splitter's face contort in agony. His own horse, stepping backward to avoid the impact, had crushed the boy's chest.

Garcia dodged the swing of a club and thrust out in answer with his lance. The point drew blood, but he knew that it was only a flesh wound. The next moment the tide of battle had swept the two apart and he lost sight of his adversary in the dust and confusion.

Still, he felt, he must find and challenge the Head Splitter chief, Gray Wolf. He was certain the other would be looking for him also. The reports of a personal vendetta had continued. Now was the time to resolve this conflict once and for all.

Across the meadow he saw two of his elk-dog soldiers charge at a tall, burly Head Splitter on one of the largest horses he had ever seen. The two made an excellent run. One or the other would certainly strike home. To his amazement, the Head Splitter was as quick as he was large. He parried the lance of one attacker with his rawhide shield, and almost simultaneously swung his war club at the other lancer. The club was longer and heavier than most, and even the glancing blow to the shoulder bowled the young rider from his horse. The youth rolled, regained his feet, and ran, left arm hanging useless as he dodged the pursuing Head Splitter.

Garcia reined his horse around and kneed her in that direction. The boys were clearly outclassed by a veteran combatant. As he moved closer, the young man gained the shelter of the broken rimrock. The pursuer abandoned the chase and reined his huge bay around to rejoin the battle. As he turned, the symbol on his painted shield became visible to Garcia for the first time. A geometrically styled design of an animal, with erect ears and a drooping tail. A wolf! He should have known. This must be Gray Wolf, the mighty warrior, real-chief of the Head Splitters.

At almost the same instant, the other seemed to recognize his sworn enemy. He roared a challenging war cry that was more of a bellow, and kneed the bay forward in a charge. The heavy war club whistled in a deadly circle as the two horses approached each other at full speed. Garcia directed the lance point at the soft midriff just below the ribs and confidently braced himself for the shock of contact.

To his complete surprise, at the last instant the other swung his shield into position. The parried lance thrust slid on past, and the shoulder of the larger horse crashed into Lolita's side. Even as he fell, a thought flitted through Garcia's mind. *She never let me down before.* The little mare rolled, but her rider had kicked free and managed to get out of her way. He was dazed and somewhat disoriented as he floundered around in the dust, trying to avoid the finishing blow he knew must be coming.

Momentum had carried the Head Splitter's horse on beyond the fallen Garcia, and now they whirled for another run. Garcia was on hands and knees in the dust. The whirling war club began to gain momentum in circles designed to finish the fight at the end of the charge. Dimly, through the dusty haze, the young man saw the big horse thundering down on him, and saw the deadly swinging club. *Is this how it happens?* he wondered. *Is this all there is to it?*

His next action was more instinct than reason. He dove directly under the front feet of the galloping bay. His reasoning, if he had any at all, was simply to put something between himself and the deadly club. The

Head Splitter would be unable to strike directly beneath his own horse. The horse unwittingly assisted, too. A horse instinctively jumps to avoid obstacles under its feet, and the big bay tucked his forefeet neatly and cleared the rolling body. Momentum carried the charge beyond, while Garcia floundered around looking for his weapon.

He heard the pounding of hooves nearing again before he grasped the lance and turned to face the enemy. His head was clearing somewhat, and he realized the definite disadvantage. He was on foot. The mobility and the long reach of the heavy club made the lance less effective. He could throw the weapon, of course, but if he missed, or the other parried the throw, he would be unarmed. By the time the charge thundered down on him again, he had reached a decision. He must kill the horse and fight the real-chief on foot.

Even so, it was with a horseman's regret that he thrust his lance deep into the soft glossy flank, jumping aside from the rush. The bay screamed and reared, nearly falling over backward, then bucking convulsively until it fell headlong. Garcia was already running forward. The impact had torn the lance from his grasp, and he snatched the knife from his belt. Gray Wolf was rising from his knees when Garcia dived headlong over the dying horse to prevent his regaining the war club.

The two rolled in the dirt, kicking, biting, gouging. The young man was amazed at the strength of the other. He's stronger than I am, Garcia thought. I've got to finish it. Gray Wolf kneed at his groin, and the dull, shocking, numbing pain drove upward toward the pit of his stomach. The Head Splitter grasped his knife wrist, and rolled on top, striving to turn the blade toward its owner.

Dully, Garcia saw the painted face looming above his, and the blade turning slowly toward his throat. In desperation, he swung a long sweeping blow with his left fist. It collided with Gray Wolf's ear, startling and confusing him. The use of fists in combat was entirely unfamiliar to the savage. Garcia struck again, and the grip loosened on his wrist. Another blow, and he wrenched the knife free and thrust upward with all his strength, in a last desperate effort of survival. The point entered the other's throat between the jawbones, and sank deep. Blood spurted over Garcia's face as he watched the eyes glaze and felt the massive weight of the warrior's body sink heavily on his chest. He lay back his head, unable to move.

Dimly, he heard shouts, and the pounding of hooves. The sounds of battle were farther away now. Someone pulled the dead Head Splitter's body away and Garcia rolled over and filled his lungs. Weakly he crawled over and sat on the dead horse, still breathing heavily.

The Head Splitters were on the run, leaving their dead behind them. A number of warriors of the People rode in hot pursuit, or flung arrows after the fleeing remnants of the attacking force. Let them go, thought Garcia. It's over. His breath still came in ragged gasps, and his belly ached. Someone spoke to him, and he looked around, to see Coyote, who had been with the bowmen among the lodges. The little man was leading

Lolita. The mare seemed uninjured, he was pleased to note. It had been a terrible impact that she had taken. Coyote handed him a heavy, blood-spattered stone war club.

"Here, Heads Off. You will want to keep this."

Garcia looked at the dead chief and shook his head, still unable to speak. He only wanted to forget the entire afternoon.

"No matter, I will keep it for you. You may want it later."

Coyote stood quietly, his presence comforting. A loose horse clopped past, reins trailing, whickering in bewilderment. Women were returning from the timber, looking for loved ones. Here and there a sudden cry, a wail of grief, and the rising notes of the mourning song.

The heaviest fighting had been in the meadow, where the horsemen had clashed, and the heaviest casualties were there. The wounded were being assisted by their friends and relatives. Garcia was still seeing the scene through a dusty red mist. This had come very close to being his last day on earth, and it had been a terrifying experience. His muscles ached, and he found that he was still unable to stand alone.

Tall One glided gracefully among the carnage and embraced him briefly.

"I am proud, my husband."

He clung to her. The girl seemed a thing of beauty, the only thing of stability in a world which had degenerated in bloody ugliness. Garcia struggled to his feet, supported by his wife and Coyote. He only wanted to go home, to lie down in the lodge and forget, in the arms of Tall One. They moved slowly in that direction.

Near the first of the lodges, a cluster of people, both men and women, crowded together in a knot. There was a sense of urgency, of extra tragedy, in the keening wails arising from this group. Some simply stood, numbly staring. Attracted by the dread fascination of the unknown, Garcia motioned, and the three altered their course. They elbowed their way into the crowd, toward the motionless figure in the center of the circle.

The dead warrior was Hump Ribs. The People of the Southern band were without a leader.

ᘉ 39 ᘊ

BY THE NEXT DAY Garcia was feeling somewhat better. He was embarrassed at his reaction to this combat situation. He felt that he had demonstrated far too much weakness.

The People did not seem to notice. He supposed they were just being kind, ignoring his faults. Besides, they were busy. The preparations for scaffold burial of the bodies of the slain went forth rapidly. The ceremonies went on all day, the entire band mourning their chief.

Preparations for the tribe to travel were also necessary. It would be imperative to move away from the stench and filth of the rotting horse carcasses. The bodies of the enemy dead were also left in the meadow.

"Let the Head Splitters care for their own dead," Coyote said casually when Garcia inquired.

On the morning of the second day after the battle, the

lodges came down, and the move began. It would soon be time for the Sun Dance. The Elk-dog band would carry perhaps the biggest news for many years. The dreaded Head Splitters had actually been met and defeated in open combat.

Thus far, there had been no major decisions requiring the judgment of a chief. Hump Ribs was sorely missed, and there was some indecisiveness apparent, but no crisis had occurred. The decision to move the tribe was an obvious one, which had required no particular planning. A new chief would be selected, Coyote said, before the band reached the Big Council. There was much talk and rumor regarding who would replace Hump Ribs as leader of the Southern band.

The logical man to succeed the chief would have been Mouse Roars, who was now dead. One of the ablest warriors was Two Pines, but the weight of political opinion was against him. His origin was in the Red Rocks, and it would be another generation before his family would be accepted as members of the Southern band. Sees Far, while extremely competent in his own specialty, had no aspirations to leadership.

There were several of the younger men who showed great promise. Standing Bird would some day be a respected chief. Some even remarked on the leadership qualities of Long Elk, son of Coyote. He had proven himself a mighty warrior in the battle, and had the wisdom and wit of his father. These young men, however, lacked the maturity and experience to ascend to the office. There was no clear choice to succeed Hump Ribs.

On the second day of travel, Garcia was walking with Coyote and White Buffalo. Coyote had suggested, after the horses became available, that the medicine man should have an elk-dog or two in recognition of his office. The old man was grateful for the new ease with which his lodge and all the artifacts of his craft could be moved. Today, he walked with Garcia and Coyote, while some of the young elk-dog men assisted in moving his lodge.

Finally, after a long silence, the medicine man spoke.

"Heads Off, I would ask something of you." He plodded along for another thirty steps or so, and then spoke again. "The men wish you to be the new chief."

Garcia was completely dumbfounded. He had expected the request to involve some question about the elk-dogs.

"Oh, no, I could not be chief," he sputtered. "I do not know the ways of the People. I am not even of the People." Such a thing was clearly ridiculous.

"Heads Off," interceded Coyote, "you have proven yourself one of the People. You are learning the ways. The young elk-dog men already know you as their leader. What more could a people ask of their chief?"

The young man resisted, but fruitlessly. Finally he agreed, grudgingly, to accept the decision of the council, if he could be assured of the continued advice of Coyote and White Buffalo.

The council was held that evening, with the medicine man presiding. If there were those opposed to this choice of leadership, they were a quiet minority. The embarrassed Garcia protested, and finally, explained to the council his need for the advice of Coyote and White Buffalo. This seemed acceptable to the others, and the council adjourned.

The new chief had little sleep that night, overwhelmed by the unwanted responsibility that had been suddenly thrust upon him. Tall One was proud and delighted, of course, and promised repeatedly to help him as the wife of a chief should. He had every confidence that her help and advice would be invaluable to him.

His immediate concern was the Big Council. Would the rest of the tribe accept an outsider as chief of the Southern band?

They arrived at the site selected for this year's Sun Dance, and the lodges were set up in the traditional place in the circle. Word of the battle had preceded them, and the members of the Southern or Elk-dog band found that they enjoyed tremendous prestige in the tribe. Were these not the People who had met and beaten the Head Splitters? Their choice of a new chief seemed almost secondary in importance. There were regrets for the loss of Hump Ribs, of course. He had been an able chief, rising in prominence. But again, had it not been a good day to die? The story would be told in song and dance for many generations.

As the night of the Big Council neared, it became obvious that the family of Heads Off intended to have him well groomed for the occasion. Coyote and Big Footed Woman came over and gave advice in his dress and grooming. Tall One carefully trimmed his beard and combed and braided his hair. She brought out a new suit of white buckskin, and new moccasins.

"You must wear or carry something that shows the strength of your medicine," advised Coyote. He looked around at the trophy war club. Garcia shook his head. He still hated the sight of the thing and allowed it in the lodge only in deference to his family's wishes.

Tall One's glance fell on her husband's armor and equipment. The graceful curves of the Spanish bit reflected the firelight as it dangled from the lodge pole. She rose and almost reverently took down the bit, the elk-dog medicine.

THE FIRE had been lighted and the People had gathered for the Big Council. Several chiefs had spoken already, but the entire tribe waited for the most important event of the evening, the speech by the new chief.

Finally, he rose in his turn. He was a handsome figure, Tall One thought, in his new white buckskins. She had put many hours of loving care into the quill-work.

On his breast hung the elk-dog medicine. The tiny silver ornaments dangled and glittered in the firelight as Lolita's Spanish bit bumped gently against the front of his shirt. He took a deep breath and tried to ignore his nervously sweating palms.

"I am Heads Off," he began in a ringing voice, "chief of the Elk-dog band of the People."

AFTERWORD

BY CHAD OLIVER

THERE IS NOTHING more "American" than the classic picture of an Indian on a horse hunting the buffalo. We have a tendency to view this scene as timeless—something that was here from time immemorial.

And yet it is not just the Europeans who once were newcomers to this land that some called the New World. The ancestors of the American Indian walked here from Asia across what is now the Bering Strait. Then, it was a landmass called Beringia. We do not know exactly how long ago that was, but it was only yesterday as geologists and archeologists measure time. There are no positively dated Indian sites older than about twelve thousand years, although there are scattered controversial finds that might double the figure. The horse evolved in the New World but became extinct here and had to be reintroduced by the Spanish. (The horse lasted long enough to have been hunted by the Indians some eight thousand years ago, but it was never domesticated by the American Indians. At that time, the great Indian civilizations that extended from Mexico to South America did not exist, and all Indians were hunters and collectors of wild plant foods.) Even the buffalo is not a true native American. Long ago, the forerunners of the buffalo (*Bison latifrons*) migrated here from Asia.

So there is a sense in which we are all strangers to

this New World of the Americas. I think that there is another way that we have become strangers to the land we live in. We are cut off from our own history for the simple reason that we have never bothered to learn it. History does not amount to a hill of beans (an American Indian crop, by the way) if it is buried in an unused library. It has to be felt, sensed, and absorbed before it can become a part of our lives.

In his Introduction to his novel, Don Coldsmith tells of finding a Spanish bit in a barrel of odds and ends in Oklahoma. This is the kind of direct contact with our past that triggers the imagination, unless we are dead from the neck up. I know how he must have felt. On our own place outside of Austin, Texas, when the rains disturb the topsoil, we turn up everything from projectile points that are several thousand years old to square rusted nails that were used by early settlers. Once, we found a woman's wedding rings, cut as though to remove it from a finger. It had a date on it, 1910, and two sets of initials. We have never been able to trace it through the records we have, but obviously there is a story behind that ring and it must be a very human one.

We don't need to wait for the rains to see the horses. My wife raises them, Arabians, and they are as much a part of our lives as the bandit-masked raccoons that feed off our front porch at night. Sometimes, because we work with them every day, we forget how remarkable it is that there are horses here at all.

It seems to me that this is really what *Trail of the Spanish Bit* is all about. It is a tale of the coming of the horse to North America, but it is more than that. It is a story that introduces us to the human beings who lived here before we did.

When Heads Off (Juan Garcia) appears among the People who would become known as the Elk-dog band, his horse is not just a strange and unknown animal. The horse was nothing less than a revolution that transformed the Plains.

Few of the historic Plains tribes lived in that area prior to the acquisition of horses. There are exceptions, such as the Blackfoot and some of the farming tribes who inhabited the river valleys, but by and large the region was sparsely populated. There are easier ways of making a living than hunting buffalo on foot. The buffalo was a notoriously unpredictable animal, despite the myth of the clockwork migrations. First you had to find the herds, then you had to get close enough to kill them with bows and arrows or spear-throwers, and then you had to transport hides and meat. Try it sometime in a flat country with sore feet.

It was the horse that changed the Plains into a hunter's paradise. When Cortes landed in Mexico in 1519, he brought with him sixteen horses—eleven stallions and five mares. (Others were brought in later, of course.) Cortes could hardly have realized the implications of what he had done, even though Bernal Diaz, who was with him during the conquest of the Aztec Empire, referred to the horses as "our only hope of survival." It took some time, and most mounted Plains tribes postdate 1700, but when horses reached the Plains in quantity there was a cultural explosion. From the Comanche in the south to the Teton Dakota (Sioux) in the north, Indians poured into the Plains. Scouting for buffalo on horseback is quite a different matter from doing it on foot. A couple of mounted hunters could kill sufficient buffalo to supply a ton of meat in ten minutes. When it came to moving lodge poles and other gear, one horse was worth a pack of dogs. It was no accident that most of the conflicts between Plains tribes involved horses. The quickest way to get horses was to raid the competition for them, which had the added advantage of cutting down on the effectiveness of your enemy. There is more than an echo of this in Coldsmith's account of the friction between the Elk-dogs and the Head Splitters. Time and time again, that is the way it was.

In the novel, the Elk-dogs adapt to the introduction of the horse rather quickly. That too has the ring of truth about it. There were Indian tribes who went from pedestrians to possibly the finest light cavalry in the world in less than a century. When you get right down to it, there is really only one explanation for this. The Indians were good with horses, and they learned fast.

When Juan Garcia first encounters the Elk-dogs, the Indians are referred to simply as the People. The name is an apt choice, and not just because most tribal names—in the Americas and elsewhere—translate out as "people" or "human beings." (This is to distinguish them, of course, from those peculiar folks who happen to live on the other side of the river.) It is a good choice because the Elk-dogs *are* people. One of the virtues of this novel is not only the merging of the identities of Juan Garcia and Heads Off but also his growing recognition that the Indians who take him in are just as human as he is.

This could not have been an easy discovery for a man of Juan Garcia's background to make. When he finds himself among the Indians, he considered them to be "miserable beggars" and "savages." There was nothing in his experience or education that would lead him to any other conclusion. Wisely, Coldsmith does not stress the humanity of the Elk-dogs by means of preaching and editorials. He shows us what these people are like in terms of specific examples. The reader is permitted to share awareness along with Juan Garcia.

As Juan Garcia comes to know them as individuals—Coyote and Big Footed Woman and Hump Ribs and White Buffalo—the stereotypes disappear and recognizable men and women emerge. As he shares their lifeway, in the beginning because he has no choice, he is forced to appreciate their wit, their courage, and their resourcefulness. The episode dealing with the broken lance point is particularly instructive in this regard.

It works the other way around, too. A man like Juan Garcia, with his horse and his armor, seemed to be a god when the Indians first saw him. He reveals his humanity quite early in the game: the god vomits, he bleeds. Soon, he is Heads Off. By the end of the book, he is one of the People. He becomes their leader, but Coldsmith makes it clear that acceptance comes before leadership.

There are details here that an anthropologist would

have handled differently, most notably in the diffusion of horses and the social structure of hunting and gathering populations. However, Don Coldsmith is a storyteller with an informed sense of history and that is a rare kind of talent.

He has put us in touch with ourselves, and the good news is that there is more to come.

We might all wish that the picture presented here had remained a true one. In *Trail of the Spanish Bit*, no matter who the leader is, the Indian and the white man were together. It is a tragedy that it could not stay that way.

Austin Texas July 1986

Center Point Publishing
600 Brooks Road • PO Box 1
Thorndike ME 04986-0001 USA

(207) 568-3717

US & Canada:
1 800 929-9108